BILLY YANK AND JOHNNY REB

SOLDIERING IN THE CIVIL WAR

Susan Provost Beller

Twenty-First Century Books • Minneapolis

This book is dedicated to those who keep Billy Yank and Johnny Reb alive—the researchers, writers, and reenactors of the Civil War.

Title page image: After a siege that lasted from June 1864 until April 1865, Union forces eventually gained control of Petersburg, Virginia, a supply center for the Confederate capital of Richmond, Virginia. Pictured in 1864 are Union soldiers of the 2nd Union Division, 9th Corps buying supplies from a sutler (a citizen who sells supplementary goods to troops).

Text copyright © 2008 by Susan Provost Beller

Twenty-First Century Books
A division of Lerner Publishing Group, Inc.
241 First Avenue North
Minneapolis, MN 55401 U.S.A.

Website address: www.lernerbooks.com

Library of Congress Cataloging-in-Publication Data

Beller, Susan Provost, 1949–
    Billy Yank and Johnny Reb : soldiering in the Civil War / by Susan Provost Beller.
        p.   cm. — (Soldiers on the battlefront)
    Includes bibliographical references and index.
    ISBN-13: 978-0-8225-6803-2 (lib. bdg. : alk. paper)
    ISBN-10: 0-8225-6803-9 (lib. bdg. : alk. paper)
    1. United States. Army—History—Civil War, 1861-1865—Juvenile literature. 2. Confederate States of America. Army—History—Juvenile literature. 3. United States. Army—Military life—History—19th century—Juvenile literature. 4. Confederate States of America. Army—Military life—Juvenile literature. 5. Soldiers—United States—History—19th century—Juvenile literature. 6. Soldiers—Confederate States of America—Juvenile literature. 7. United States—History—Civil War, 1861-1865—Personal narratives—Juvenile literature. I. Title.
    E607.B44 2008
    973.7'4—dc22   2006010240

Manufactured in the United States of America
1 2 3 4 5 6 — JR — 13 12 11 10 09 08

Contents

The Civil War (1861–1865) would have many other names, including the War Between the  States, the Second War for Independence, Mr. Lincoln's War, and the War of the Rebellion. These other names reflect whether a person lives in the North or the South. Historians debate the reasons for the Civil War. But no matter what triggered the conflict—differences on slavery, economics, states' rights, a way of life—the war probably was destined to happen.

Instead of an analysis of the reasons for the war, here is the real-life world of Billy Yank and Johnny Reb, told in their own words. Billy Yank was how a Union (Northern) soldier was commonly referred to. Johnny Reb was the nickname given to Confederate (Southern) soldiers. For soldiers on both sides, the Civil War was the most memorable event of their lives. Their memoirs tell not just the exciting moments of battles. They also reveal the boredom of camp, the tedium of drill, and the daily complaints about bad food, bad camp conditions, and disease.

"There is so much suffering here that it is good to know that there are some dear ones at home safe and free from pain. We have had some fearful fighting, have lost a great many men in killed wounded and missing. . . . May you never see the sights I have seen for the last week." George Barton wrote these words to his mother and sister in 1864 during the horrible Battle of the Wilderness, a battle that took place in a desolate area of Virginia called the Wilderness. The words of the Union and Confederate soldiers, recorded in their letters or diaries, capture the real horrors of what it was like to be a soldier on either side during the war.

Of course, not all the letters, diaries, and reminiscences are available. Some have been lost, and some are still hidden away in attics. Some were never written because not all soldiers could read and write. Many stories, such as those of the African American soldiers who served in the "Colored" regiments, are lost in the past. Even though we may not be able to represent fully some groups of soldiers, the memoirs we do have are a vitally important part of the Civil War story. In all, only a very small percentage of the soldiers have left us their memories. We can only wonder at all the great accounts we will never get to read.

In this book, we will hear from a number of Billy Yanks and Johnny Rebs. But the focus will be on two representative soldiers. Billy Yank Theodore Gerrish is a Union soldier from the 20th Maine Regiment. Johnny Reb Carlton McCarthy is a member of the Richmond Howitzers.

> *"Everything was new and exciting to my boyish vision."*
>
> —Theodore Gerrish, 1862

CHAPTER ONE

SIGNING UP

"The Confederate soldier," wrote Johnny Reb Carlton McCarthy, "was a venerable old man, a youth, a child, a preacher, a farmer, merchant, student, statesman, orator, father, brother, husband, son—the wonder of the world, the terror of his foes!" The same might be said of his Union counterpart, Billy Yank. This fight between the North and the South—the Union and the Confederacy—pitted men against one another who had much in common and were eager to be part of the adventure of a lifetime.

At the beginning of the war at least, men had great enthusiasm for signing up. It would be a war of the young. About 2,700,000 soldiers fought for the Union, while another 1 million fought for the Confederacy. The

Johnny Reb Carlton McCarthy was from Richmond, Virginia. He left behind letters and memoirs that gave detailed accounts of what soldiering was like during the Civil War.

numbers vary among historians. But most would agree that of the 2,700,000 Union soldiers, more than 2 million were under the age of twenty-one. About 1 million were eighteen or younger. Even these numbers were only the official ones. Younger soldiers, desperate not to miss out on their chance to fight, often enlisted under age. A piece of paper with a number 18 written on it and placed in his shoe allowed a youth to swear under oath that he was "over 18" without violating his conscience. One soldier, Joseph Bushong, claimed to have been in the army for three full years before he turned eighteen. He said that the lie he gave about his age was "the only lie I ever told in my life."

THE BLUE AND THE GRAY

Among the other names given to the Union and Confederate soldiers are the Blue and the Gray. The names come from the colors of their uniforms. As with many commonly known "facts," this one is not entirely true. When the war opened with the First Battle of Bull Run (1861) in Manassas, Virginia, nothing was uniform about the uniforms worn by either side. In fact, the numerous different colors and flags used by the troops may have actually caused the North to lose the battle. A Union unit thought some approaching soldiers were on their side and didn't open fire until it was too late. The advancing troops were actually Confederates. It was only after Manassas that new flags and uniforms were designed to avoid such confusion in battle.

The Union did decide to wear blue uniforms. However, the Confederacy dressed its soldiers in uniforms that weren't really that gray. Their official color was butternut, a sort of brownish gray color that was created with homemade dyes. With new standardized uniforms, the opposing forces could be distinguished from one another in battle. Fortunately for history, their representative names didn't entirely match their actual uniform colors. The Blue and the Butternut doesn't sound quite so impressive.

SOLDIERS' ORIGINS

Not only were the soldiers young, they were also often immigrants or sons of immigrants. They enlisted mostly for the Union and were willing to preserve the country that had given them a new home. A large number of German regiments came from their settlements in New York, Ohio, Missouri, Pennsylvania, Wisconsin, and Illinois. The Irish also provided great numbers of soldiers, perhaps the most famous being those who made up the Irish Brigade.

But regiments of French, Spaniards, Italians, Scots, Swedes, Norwegians,

This 1860s photo of a group of soldiers from the Civil War shows that some were very young and from various backgrounds.

Swiss, Welsh, Dutch, and Mexicans also fought for the Union. Many more immigrants had settled in the North than in the South, but the Confederacy was also represented by its immigrant population. Irish and French were the two largest groups to enlist, but many soldiers were of Italian, German, Polish, Spanish, or Mexican background.

About half the soldiers on both sides were farmers. Laborers and carpenters made up another large group. But most occupations—shoemakers, surveyors, blacksmiths, wheelwrights, butchers, masons, mechanics, merchants, even teachers, doctors, and lawyers—were represented. The soldiers came from all the states then in the Union. Soldiers from the North fought for the Confederacy just as soldiers from the South fought for the Union. Tiny Vermont provided the greatest number of soldiers per capita (based on population) to the Union.

SOLDIERS OF COLOR

African American soldiers also fought for both the Union and the Confederacy. But their roles were somewhat different from those of the other soldiers fighting in the Civil War. From the very beginning, African American orator Frederick Douglass encouraged President Abraham Lincoln to enlist African American soldiers: "The arm of the slave [is] the best defense against the arm of the slaveholder." But African American units didn't appear in the field for the Union until 1863, after Lincoln issued the Emancipation Proclamation, which freed all slaves in the Confederate states.

Initially, the white officers and white soldiers didn't respect these units. African American soldiers were often assigned only menial tasks. They were paid a salary of $10 (about $137 in modern money) per month, instead of the $13 ($178) per month of the white Billy Yank. They received no clothing allowance for their uniforms.

Over time, African American soldiers earned the respect of the white soldiers for their bravery in battle, especially for their actions at Fort Wagner, Fort Pillow, and Fort Hudson. About 180,000 African Americans served in the Union army in 166 African American regiments. About two-thirds of them had escaped from the South. But throughout the war, they mostly remained under the command of white officers. About one hundred African American soldiers eventually became officers, but none ranked higher than captain.

The Confederate army used African Americans from the very beginning, but not as soldiers. Initially, slaves were brought in as laborers to take care of the camps. Sometimes they were made to work

At first black soldiers were not well received by white soldiers and officers, but eventually organized units appeared in the field and earned respect. Here, twenty-seven Union soldiers of Company E, 4th U.S. Colored Infantry, pose with rifles at the end of the war at Fort Lincoln in Washington, D.C.

at gunpoint and were even put in danger by being exposed to gunfire from Union troops. Some white officers from the South, such as General Patrick R. Cleburne, argued to have the African Americans serve as regular soldiers. He even suggested that those who served this way should earn their freedom. But most Southerners would have agreed with Confederate General Howell Cobb that "the day you make a soldier of them is the beginning of the end of the revolution. . . . If slaves seem [like] good soldiers, then our whole theory of slavery is wrong." It wasn't until near the very end of the war in 1865 that Confederate president Jefferson Davis finally ordered the recruitment of African American soldiers to serve in the Confederate army.

One exception to this policy existed in the South. In March 1862, a group of "free persons of color" in New Orleans, Louisiana, formed a regiment called the Native Guards. When Union troops captured the city, the Native Guards remained and offered their services to the Union.

Native Americans also fought as Billy Yanks and Johnny Rebs during the Civil War. At the Battle of

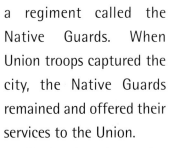

Recruiting officers swear in two Native American Civil War recruits in 1861.

Cherokee Stand Watie, a general in the Confederate army, was the highest-ranking Native American of the Civil War. This portrait was taken after the war.

Pea Ridge in Arkansas in 1862, Native Americans fought against one another. The Confederate government actively recruited the services of the Native Americans. Degataga, a Cherokee also known as Stand Watie, organized a regiment to serve the South. By the end of the war, he was a general, the highest-ranking Native American in either army. On June 23, 1865, he finally surrendered his forces to the Union. His was "the last surrender of a fighting force by a general of the Confederate armies," according to one historian. About 3,500 Native Americans fought for the Union. Lieutenant Colonel Ely Parker, a Seneca, served on General Grant's personal staff from the Vicksburg campaign in 1863 until the end of the war.

WOMEN IN THE WAR

Even though the soldiers were nicknamed Billy Yanks and Johnny Rebs, more than a few were Betty Yanks and Jane Rebs. Mary Livermore recorded the work of the Sanitary Commission after the war. She estimated that about four hundred women dressed and fought as men for the Union during the conflict. Some were wives who snuck into the army to be with their husbands. Others were just girls and women who were determined to be part of the great adventure. Many were discovered and sent home, but some actually fought throughout the entire war.

The stories of these female soldiers are not widely known. But long before the woman's suffrage movement, women were showing their patriotism by dying for their country. Union general William Hays sent in a report on the burial of dead soldiers after the Battle of Gettysburg in July 1863. His troops buried 1,629 bodies—387 Union soldiers and 1,242 Confederates. He noted that a Confederate body was "one female (private), in rebel uniform." Not all the women served as privates, either. At least one served as a Confederate lieutenant and another as a major in the Union army.

Rosetta Wakeman—who served under the name Lyons Wakeman with the 153rd New York Volunteers—wrote home that she was "enjoying myself first rate." She wrote regularly, signing her letters with her real name. She assured everyone that she loved the work of soldiering and was not afraid to die: "If it is God['s] will for me to be killed here, it is my will to die." As a prison guard, she wrote that she knew of a woman who was being held in prison for breaking the

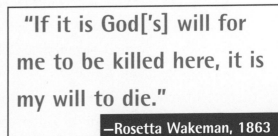

"If it is God['s] will for me to be killed here, it is my will to die."
—Rosetta Wakeman, 1863

"regulation of war" by leading her troops into battle. Rosetta Wakeman excitedly wrote: "When the Rebels bullets was acoming like a hail storm she rode her horse and gave orders to the men." Rosetta Wakeman did not survive the war, dying of dysentery after a long hospital stay in 1864. No mention was made that she was a woman. Historians guess that perhaps she held on to her secret to the very end. She was buried as Lyons Wakeman in New Orleans, where she had died.

The Civil War was a great adventure for all the soldiers. One of the most striking features in the letters, diaries, and reminiscences is the awareness that this was the most exciting time of their lives. Rosetta Wakeman was not the only one enjoying herself. Billy Yank Theodore Gerrish wrote: "Everything was new and exciting to

During the Civil War, Rosetta Wakeman disguised herself and served as a man, Private Lyons Wakeman.

my boyish vision." His Confederate counterpart, Johnny Reb Carlton McCarthy, looking back after the war, could still write that for all of them, "the deadly struggle marked a grand period in their history!"

> **"An untrained drum corps furnished us with music; each musician kept different time, and each man in the regiment took a different step. . . . "**
>
> —Theodore Gerrish, 1862

CHAPTER TWO

BECOMING A SOLDIER

"The first thing in the morning is drill, then drill, then drill again. Then drill, drill, a little more drill. Then drill, and lastly drill. Between drills, we drill and sometimes stop to eat a little and have a roll-call." Oliver W. Norton of the 83rd Pennsylvania Regiment captured perfectly Billy Yank and Johnny Reb's feelings about drill. It was the most complained-about part of the soldier's day. Along with the food, drilling was the part of the soldier's life about which they most often wrote home. The soldiers, both Union and Confederate, could not understand the purpose of daily drills.

They had enlisted and left home eager to fight. But instead of meeting their enemies in battle and defeating them, all they did was drill—company drill, regimental drill, brigade drill, division drill. They recognized that some drilling was necessary. Theodore Gerrish of the 20th Maine Regiment wrote of his regiment's pathetic attempt at

Billy Yanks and Johnny Rebs all agreed that continuous drills were the most tedious part of the soldier's day. Here Union soldiers stand at attention in a photo taken by well-known Civil War photographer Mathew Brady.

order as they marched into Washington in September 1862 to join the war: "It was a most ludicrous march. We had never been drilled, and we felt that our reputation was at stake. An untrained drum corps furnished us with music; each musician kept different time, and each man in the regiment took a different step. Old soldiers sneered; the people laughed and cheered; we marched, ran, walked, galloped, and stood still, in our vain endeavor to keep step."

Theirs was not the only regiment to need drill to march like soldiers. But from the soldiers' point of view, they were drilled much too often. The officers thought otherwise. And the experience of both the Northern and Southern armies in the First Battle of Bull Run on July 21, 1861, proved that all the drill so far had been far from enough.

The Confederates defeated General Irvin McDowell and his Union troops at the war's first major battle at Manassas, Virginia, on July 21, 1861.

FIRST BATTLE

Abraham Lincoln had encouraged Union general Irvin McDowell to meet the rebels in battle at Manassas, near Washington, D.C. The troops were mostly ninety-day troops, and their enlistment period was almost up. McDowell argued that the soldiers had not had enough training to fight a major battle. He said his troops were still too green. But Lincoln responded: "You are green, it is true, but they are green also; you are green alike."

No one could have predicted what actually happened when this order was obeyed. Everyone on both sides had projected that this

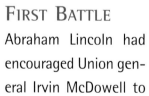

conflict was going to be a one-battle war. The armies would meet. A battle would be fought. Northerners thought the Union would win. The Confederates believed a Southern man was worth more than three Union soldiers. They felt that their side would be victorious. Whoever won, peace would be negotiated after this single battle. So everyone wanted the chance to be present at the battle of a lifetime. Soldiers had hurried to enlist, fearing they would miss the fight. And as the battle neared, the citizens of Washington also wanted to be sure to have front-row seats for the spectacle. McDowell had to contend not only with green troops but also with civilians. Many packed their picnic baskets and headed to the countryside in their carriages, as if this was the greatest social event of the year.

Reluctantly, McDowell moved his army to meet the Confederates. He noted with disgust that "they stopped every moment to pick blackberries or get water; they would not keep in the ranks, order as much as you pleased." Manassas was a hard-fought battle. At several points in the conflict, it looked as if either the Union or Confederates were about to win. In the end, the Confederates were victorious.

At the end of the battle, McDowell would report: "The men having thrown away their haversacks in the battle and left them behind, they are without food. . . . The larger part of the men are a confused mob, entirely demoralized." Others would defend the actions of the soldiers: "There was no general demoralization in the army, although many of the troops acted like all novices in the dreadful art of war, and executed some movements with great confusion."

However one interpreted the actions of Billy Yank that day, leadership on both sides of the conflict saw it as a near disaster. Billy Yank and Johnny Reb would experience more drilling before the armies could meet in battle again.

CITIZEN-SOLDIERS GO TO WAR

Blame for the 1861 Union loss at Manassas was placed on any number of bad decisions. However, most of them could be grouped together under the category of problems encountered when trying to transform citizens into soldiers.

At the beginning of the war, the United States had a standing army of seventeen thousand soldiers. Only two generals in this army had ever commanded an army on the battlefield. As the Southern states seceded (withdrew) from the Union, two-thirds of the officers left the U.S. Army to join the Confederacy. The South had a stronger military tradition than the North did. Many well-to-do Southerners sent their sons to military schools, such as the Citadel and the Virginia Military Institute (VMI). However, even in the South, the Civil War would be fought by citizens who became soldiers, not by soldiers who had chosen the military as a career.

The response to the call for volunteers was fantastic on both sides. Young men hurriedly signed up for ninety-days' service to avoid missing the war. They were untrained, mostly farm boys. In many cases, their officers knew no more about the military and fighting than the recruits did. Recruits on both sides believed strongly that they were free citizens. They were willing to defend their country but also felt entitled to their constitutional rights. Unfortunately, the nature of war doesn't allow for military decisions to be made with a democratic process among the soldiers. Even the officers were often unwilling to accept orders from their superiors. The citizen-soldiers, in both the North and the South, would have to learn to be soldiers. They'd have to accept drill, discipline, and the need for a chain of command if they were to succeed as an effective army.

REALITY CHECK

The soldiers of both sides would also have to accept the reality of being soldiers. They would have to learn to follow orders. The indignant words of Private Johnny Haley of the 17th Maine spoke for most of the Billy Yanks and Johnny Rebs. "How strange it seems to us who have enjoyed our freedom so recently to be thus deprived of all privileges. Have we enlisted to secure freedom for others only to give up our own?"

Billy Yank John Haley of the 17th Maine, photographed in January 1863

But the realities of military life meant that men did indeed have to give up much of their personal freedom to become effective soldiers. Wrote Johnny Reb Carlton McCarthy, "It took years to teach the educated privates in the army that it was their duty to give unquestioning obedience to officers because they were such, who were awhile ago their playmates and associates in business." Billy Yank Theodore Gerrish observed the same about his fellow soldiers: "One of the most difficult things in the world for a genuine Yankee to do, was to settle down, and become accustomed to the experience of a soldier's life. He was naturally inquisitive, and wanted to know all the reasons why an order was given, before he could obey it."

Not only privates had that difficulty. One of the problems at Manassas had been the unwillingness of regimental officers on both sides to accept orders from their own higher-ranking officers. Each officer seemed to want to conduct war as he alone saw fit. Billy

Yanks like Theodore Gerrish could comment bitterly on the "couple of gilt straps upon the shoulders of one who at home was far beneath him" that made him into an officer. The officers themselves were also too conscious of their rank and were reluctant to take orders from anyone.

The drill of the future would not be just for the soldiers of individual regiments. It would involve regiments, brigades, and divisions until the whole army, officers and men, had learned to move as one. With the first major battle over, Billy Yank and Johnny Reb would learn to become soldiers. Johnny Reb Carlton McCarthy's comment on the Confederate soldier really fit both sides: "The Confederate soldier was peculiar in that he was ever ready to fight, but never ready to submit to the routine duty and discipline of the camp or on the march." Billy Yank Theodore Gerrish also described both when he wrote of the Union soldier: "Accustomed to be independent, the words *go* and *come* grated harshly upon his ear."

Before the two armies met again in battle, Billy Yank and Johnny Reb would have countless drills to prepare them to do a much better job than they had at Manassas. By the time the war was in its second year, discipline would become a way of life for them. The soldiers would have heard *go* and *come* enough times that obeying orders would become second nature.

> "We are now in a fine place. It is in a pine woods. We have built up our tents with logs so that they are very nice and warm. . . ."
>
> —Thomas Owen, 1863

CHAPTER THREE

LIFE IN CAMP

"Another fancy idea was that the principal occupation of a soldier should be actual conflict with the enemy. They did not dream of such a thing as camping for six months at a time without firing a gun, or marching and countermarching to mislead the enemy, or driving wagons and ambulances, building bridges, currying horses, and the thousand commonplace duties of the soldier." Johnny Reb Carlton McCarthy's description is very accurate. Some Billy Yanks and Johnny Rebs served through the entire Civil War and never were involved in a major battle. Even Billy Yanks and Johnny Rebs whose careers included a great deal of fighting spent the overwhelming amount of their time either in camp, on guard duty, or on the march.

Aside from drill or guard duty, life in camp revolved around cooking and eating, improving housing, recreation, and letters from home. Cooking and eating were big topics. Along with complaints about drill, food issues were the most written-about items in letters home.

HOME AWAY FROM HOME

Billy Yank and Johnny Reb spent a lot of their free time improving their living arrangements. This was especially true as winter neared. The soldiers knew that they most likely would not be fighting until the spring. The effort to create comfortable winter quarters became a major focus of their lives. Union soldier Thomas Owen from New York wrote home in January 1863: "We are now in a fine place. It is in a pine woods. We have built up our tents with logs so that they are very nice and warm. . . . Think some of moving soon, which don't please us much now that we have such a nice place." The next winter, he was bragging "We are fixing up good winter quarters." That "good winter quarters" could make a difference in Billy Yank's attitude is reflected in Owen's letter home a few months later. "Tell her not to worry about me in the least for I am well and have comfortable quarters.

These Union soldiers kept busy continually trying to improve their winter quarters so that they could remain comfortable while they weren't fighting. Mathew Brady took this photo during the war.

Some of the winter quarters became quite elaborate. This village was built by the Confederate Army at Manassas, Virginia, in 1862.

Very good living. In fact, I am enjoying myself."

Johnny Reb McCarthy gives his own account of the soldier's attempt to create a home away from home. He talked of the soldiers' excitement as they learned they were about to go into winter quarters. "Hasty plans for comfort and convenience are eagerly discussed till late into the night, and await only the dawn of another day for execution." McCarthy goes on to discuss the various styles of winter quarters developed by the soldiers. He devotes several pages in his memoir to the process of settling down for the winter. There is no mistaking the enthusiasm of this Johnny Reb for setting up just the right camp.

Once settled into a camp, Billy Yank and Johnny Reb turned

their thoughts to recreation and the comforts they missed from home. Carlton McCarthy described being in winter quarters as "a good time to make and carve beautiful pipes of hard wood with horn mouth-pieces, very comfortable chairs, bread trays, haversacks, and a thousand other conveniences."

Many of the recreational items created were for personal use. But sometimes the soldiers undertook elaborate building projects in winter quarters. A group of soldiers belonging to the Irish Brigade built themselves a church. Peter Welsh wrote home about the finished product: "The 88th have an enclosure mad[e] in front of the chaplins [chaplain's] tent with ceder [cedar] bushes and that forms the church with the little alter [altar] in the tent inside." A Rhode Island unit of Billy Yanks built log cabins for their officers and then a church that even included a fireplace and a chandelier made out of tin cans!

LEISURE TIME

Once settled into camp and when not drilling or eating, some soldiers amused themselves with dice games and smoking their clay pipes. Drunkenness was sometimes a problem for the bored soldiers in camp, and good officers kept the men busy. Officers also tried to arrange religious services to keep trouble in the camps to a minimum. But, considering the number of soldiers, the problems were fairly minimal. Johnny Reb McCarthy captured the life of the soldier in camp this way: "He played marbles, spun his top, played at football, bandy [kind of like ice hockey], and hop-scotch; slept quietly, rose early, and had a good appetite, and was happy. He had time now comfortably to review the toils, dangers, and hardships of the past campaign."

According to Billy Yank Theodore Gerrish, the soldier also had

These off-duty drummer boys kept themselves entertained and out of trouble by playing cards and other games. Drummer boys, who were often quite young, played music for the soldiers while on the march.

time for "the practical, good-natured jokes we used to practice upon each other." He tells of such pranks as distracting the cook so the soldiers could grab more than their share of food. But he seems to most enjoy the story of the picket post. Apparently, a new recruit arrived and was concerned that he would not know what to do when assigned picket duty (guarding the camp boundaries at night). Gerrish led the others as they convinced the recruit that picket duty was performed standing on top of a small pointed post. From this position, they explained, the soldier had a good view of the surrounding area. Then Gerrish created a post on which the recruit could practice standing. The poor recruit tried for hours to balance on the post. Much later, an officer came by and advised him about

THE SLEEPING SOLDIER WHOM LINCOLN PARDONED

Sleeping while on guard duty is considered one of the most serious offenses that a soldier can commit in time of war. Army regulations stated that such a soldier deserves to be put to death because of the risk he brought upon his fellow soldiers. On August 31, 1861, Private William Scott *(pictured right)* from the 3rd Vermont volunteered to serve picket duty for a friend. He fell asleep while on duty and was awakened by the officer of the guard. Found guilty at his court-martial (military trial), he was sentenced to be shot for his dereliction of duty. It was still early in the war, and William Scott had been in the army for only six weeks. He would be the first soldier of the war to be executed.

The death sentence shocked the nation. Many felt that it was a terrible injustice. Others, including editorialists for the *New York Times*, felt it was just and would serve to warn other soldiers to do their duty. Fortunately for William Scott, President Abraham Lincoln was one of those who felt he should not die for his act. Lincoln acknowledged that he did not wish to undermine "the discipline of the army," but that he felt mercy should be shown this one time. William Scott had been pardoned. His grateful father traveled to Washington, D.C., to thank the president in person. William Scott returned to duty. The following spring, on April 16, 1862, Scott fought in the front line of Vermonters attacking a position at Lee's Mills, Virginia, and was killed in battle.

how picket duty was really performed. Gerrish counted it as one of their most successful pranks.

The most cherished activity for both Billy Yank and Johnny Reb revolved around writing letters home and receiving and reading their mail. Union officer Elisha Rhodes from Rhode Island captured the soldier's need for word from home very well in his diary entry for March 6, 1865. "We have received no mail for several days and do not like it. A soldier can do without hard bread but not without his letters from home." Peter Welsh of the 28th Massachusetts had a similar complaint in a letter home. "I have not received any letter from you for over a month allthough I have wrote several letters to you since." Theodore Gerrish spoke sadly and movingly of those who didn't receive any letters. Mail was important since "each letter received was like a messenger from home, and was an additional cord binding our hearts to our loved ones."

On the other hand, at times the messages from home could be painful. Some African American Union soldiers came from border states that still had slave populations. They worried that their families might face harassment from the slaveowners in the community. Imagine the distress of the soldier receiving the following letter from home. "I have had nothing but trouble since you left. You recollect what I told you how they would do after you was gone. They abuse me because you went . . . and beat me scandalously the day before yesterday. . . . You ought not to left me in the fix I am in & all these little helpless children to take care of."

> ❝We were very short of rations. We had not had a bean or any salt pork . . . for a month."
>
> —William Bircher, 1863

CHAPTER FOUR

FOOD

For Billy Yank and Johnny Reb, the most significant benefit of a long stay in camp was that the food—the most important part of a soldier's life—was better and more plentiful than when they were on the march. "Our rations were for the most part good and plenty of it . . . hard tac . . . that sometimes had to be broken with your heel or musket. Soft bread when in a permanent camp. Fresh beef. Salt junk (pork). Salt horse (beef). Peas. Beans. Potatoes. Desecated [desiccated] vegetables. Rice etc." said Alfred Bellard from New Jersey. He was not unhappy with the rations fed to soldiers in the Union army. However, it was much more common to hear negative comments than to hear his fair assessment.

Johnny Reb Carlton McCarthy was less generous in his description of the Confederate rations. "Sometimes there was an abundant issue of bread, and no meat; then meat in any quantity, and no flour or meal; sugar in abundance, and no coffee to be had for 'love or money;' and then coffee in plenty, without a grain of sugar."

Supplying soldiers with rations when they needed them was a

A sutler's tent draws a crowd of hungry soldiers during the siege of Petersburg, Virginia (1864–1865).

nightmare for the quartermasters in both armies. When the armies were in camp, the job was done adequately enough to keep Billy Yank and Johnny Reb at least reasonably content. But, as the war progressed, Johnny Reb increasingly had to do with half rations and sometimes none at all. However, most of the war was fought on Southern soil. So Johnny Reb received a great deal of food from Southerners who were more than happy to show their support. Billy Yank, on the other hand, had the advantage of sutlers' wagons. These wagons, supplied by civilians, followed behind the troops and did a wonderful business (especially right after the soldiers received their pay!). Sutlers supplied supplementary goods such as cakes and pies and better food.

In spite of the best efforts of the quartermasters, however, complaints about food in the letters home are extremely common. Countless are the descriptions of hardtack that was inedible even after soaking and meat covered with maggots. Some complained that food issued to the regiment never got past the officers' mess.

FOOD ON THE MARCH

The real food hardships, especially for Billy Yank, came when he was on the march. Orders were routinely given forbidding foraging in the countryside. Soldiers were often severely punished if they broke those commands. But the inability to keep the marching army supplied caused many complaints to be sent home. The worst cases were on the western front (the Mississippi and Tennessee river regions). In this area, the war was waged over a much larger area. The supplying communities were quite far away. Union drummer William Bircher from Minnesota recorded his disgust with the food situation in his diary in 1863. "We were very short of rations. We had not had a bean or any salt pork issued us for a month, and with those articles cut off from the soldiers' bill of fare life was not worth living, and patriotism and love of country must take second place."

Numerous letters and diaries record how important food was to the soldiers. African Americans often served as the cooks.

SHARING WITH THE ENEMY

The lack of food led to a great deal of barter between Billy Yank and Johnny Reb, even though officers disapproved. When the armies were camped near each other, the exchange of goods by the soldiers became rather common. Johnny Reb had tobacco, increasingly rare in the North since it was grown in the South. Billy Yank, of course, had food. The two sides seemed quite capable of exchanging items at night and then fighting each other the following morning.

As the Civil War progressed, the story for Johnny Reb became one of near starvation. The effectiveness of the Northern blockade of Southern ports, along with the inflation that sent prices skyrocketing, helped to cause real scarcity. Severe hunger was felt throughout the South. In fact, the soldiers probably ate better than some of the people living in the big cities such as Richmond, Virginia. But the soldiers often supplemented their food in a gruesome way. After battle, it was not uncommon for Johnny Reb to pick through the pockets and haversacks of the dead and wounded for something edible.

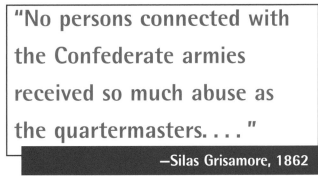

"No persons connected with the Confederate armies received so much abuse as the quartermasters. . . . "

—Silas Grisamore, 1862

The food situation became critical. By July 1863, some Confederate units were officially informed that their mules could be killed. Mule meat was given to the soldiers for their rations. Some food items that were supposed to be part of the Confederate soldiers' rations, such as coffee, became impossible to find.

QUARTERMASTER McKINLEY

One of the Union's quartermasters was William McKinley *(below)*. He was part of the 23rd regiment of Ohio Volunteer Infantry. His commander was Colonel Rutherford B. Hayes. Both men would later become presidents of the United States.

McKinley keenly realized that their ability to fight was partly based on his ability to feed them. In fact, at the Battle of Antietam in Maryland in 1862, the Union soldiers left for the battlefield without having had breakfast. Over the course of the fighting, the soldiers weakened. McKinley risked his life—and the lives of a couple of mules—to bring hot food to the men. They met his efforts with loud cheers. Colonel Hayes remarked, "From his hands every man in the regiment was served with hot coffee and warm meats, a thing that had never occurred under similar circumstances in any other army in the world."

Billy Yank and Johnny Reb may have found much cause for grievances about their provisions, but pity their quartermasters. Confederate quartermaster Silas Grisamore probably expressed the feelings of quartermasters on both sides when he wrote: "No persons connected with the Confederate armies received so much abuse as the quartermasters.... Let forage be plenty or scarce, let the roads be good or bad, let the sun shine or the rain fall, subsistence had to be procured, provisions transported."

> **They had been left to us as a legacy, and were the sole inhabitants of the huts that had been evacuated by the routed enemy."**
>
> —Irish Brigade chaplain Father William Corby, 1862

CHAPTER FIVE

DIRT AND DISEASE

"Looking at the shirt I had just removed, I found it full all of— excuse the word— clothes lice, or 'greybacks.'... It is easy to laugh about this now, but sensitive persons fairly shudder at the thought of this pestilence, worse in nature than many of the Egyptian plagues." Irish Brigade chaplain Father William Corby wrote about this problem after taking over a Confederate encampment after the Peninsula campaign in Virginia in 1862. "They had been left to us as a legacy, and were the sole inhabitants of the huts that had been evacuated by the routed enemy."

At least one Johnny Reb disagreed with who brought the graybacks to whom. "The grayback was never here until Lincoln's soldiers came, and the easy presumption is that they brought him along with them and turned him loose on us. Did not the Yankees bring the chicken cholera, the hog cholera, women-in-breeches, and various other pests and plagues?" Corby's encounter with graybacks was only

Father Corby *(seated, far right)* was chaplain of the Irish Brigade. His memoirs give a picture of the difficulties of soldiering during the Civil War.

one of the annoying and often even deadly parts of camp life.

DEATH BY DISEASE

Billy Yank and Johnny Reb faced a life not only of bad food but also of poor sanitary conditions. Two out of every three deaths in the Civil War were from disease, not from battle wounds. Billy Yank Theodore Gerrish captured the sadness of these numbers. He wrote, "There is some inspiration to die in the shock of conflict, amidst the crash of contending hosts, to pass away in a whirlwind of fire; but there is no satisfaction in struggling with disease, and to grow weak and shadowy under its touch, and to know from the beginning that death is the only relief."

Reporting on camp conditions during the war, Union doctor Roberts Bartholow wrote about the recruits' arrival in camp.

> *As soon after enlistment as possible, the recruit is hurried to the depot; he is supplied with army rations badly cooked and uncleanly served; he is drilled vigorously several hours each day; at night, furnished with one or two blankets and occasionally a little straw, he is thrust into a tent with a large number of others, or into crowded temporary quarters, where he is subjected to horribly impure air, frequently to cold and dampness, and always to excessive discomfort, or he is required to perform a tour of guard duty which interrupts his habit of nightly repose; but slender opportunities of washing and bathing are afforded him, and he is at all times exposed to the influences of the unwholesome air of badly-policed camps and quarters, and to the emanations from his comrades suffering under various contagious maladies.*

In fact, new troops arriving at the camps often found their first battle to be against measles, mumps, and other diseases. Living together in large groups for the first time, the soldiers shared their germs with others around them. Only after this process of toughening up were the survivors trained to fight.

After having survived the early exposure to measles, the recruits moved on to the more common problems of camp life. Dysentery, also called diarrhea, was an almost constant companion of the soldiers. No one knew why some regiments were healthier than others. Doctors explored all sorts of theories to prevent dysentery. One doctor even recommended that drinking the blood of a freshly killed animal would prevent diarrhea.

POOR MEDICAL CARE

Billy Yank Theodore Gerrish gave the soldier's perspective on camp conditions. "The men were unused to the climate, the exposure, and the food, so that the whole experience was in direct contrast to their life at home." But he saved his greatest disgust for the hospitals where sick soldiers had to go for treatment: "The buildings used as hospitals were but illy adapted to such a purpose, being very imperfect in ventilation, cleanliness, and general convenience." Gerrish shared the common soldier's fear of the medical treatment they would receive if they reported an illness. Like many other soldiers, he preferred to stay in the care of his friends rather than go to the regimental hospitals. In fact, looking back with modern medical knowledge, the key to health was proper sanitation. Sometimes something as simple as making sure the latrines did not foul the drinking water could have saved lives and prevented dysentery.

Regimental hospitals frequently were little more than a few tents. This photo is of the hospital of the 12th Vermont.

African American soldiers had even more cause to worry about their medical care than Gerrish did. Few white doctors were willing to serve with the African American regiments. One historian notes that "as a result, hospital stewards were appointed to the posts of assistant surgeon and surgeon in the African American regiments, where they performed many duties for which they were not qualified, including surgery." Although an attempt was made to fix the situation, he notes that "the lack of adequate medical care in the African American regiments persisted to the end of the war."

PERSONAL HABITS

Personal cleanliness was another issue. This was true even in regiments where sanitation was good and disease rates were low, such as the 2nd Rhode Island Volunteers. The captain of this regiment wrote about the misery of not having had a chance to change his clothes during five weeks of heavy marching and fighting. Many of the soldiers didn't have additional clothing. They would go for months without the opportunity to get clean. They would suffer from "long, tedious marches under a scorching sun, with dust penetrating every particle of . . . clothing, or under pelting rain and through mud knee-deep," in the words of Father Corby. Letters home and diaries speak of their exhaustion from marches that denied them real rest for several days in a row. Often they would stop for the night. But their supply wagons hadn't kept up. So the soldiers had no food and tents. They'd sleep in the cold and mud only to face another long day of marching in the morning.

The dirt and the bad food were problems. But days of hunger alternating with times of gorging when food became available again didn't help. The lack of personal cleanliness and the use of impure drinking water were common. Doctors, however, were actually pleased with the disease rate of only 60 percent. In the Mexican War (1846–1848), 88 percent of the deaths had been from disease.

> **"No pen can describe the sufferings and physical exhaustion of an army of infantry marching thirty miles a day."**
>
> —Theodore Gerrish, 1862

ON THE MARCH

CHAPTER SIX

William Bircher was only fifteen years old when he joined the 2nd Regiment, Minnesota Veteran Volunteers, as their drummer boy in 1861. Bircher kept a detailed diary of his years as a Union soldier. Each day he recorded the weather and the number of miles that he marched. He also added information on what happened that day. At the end of each year, he totaled the number of miles he'd marched. The totals were shocking. In 1862 the total was 1,493 miles. The year 1863 was a good one for the unit, with only 917 miles of marching. But in 1864, the Minnesota soldiers marched an incredible 2,689 miles. Many, many entries in Bircher's diary recorded marches of more than 20 miles.

John Lincoln Clem *(left)* was only eleven years old when he joined the Union army as a drummer boy.

Both Billy Yank and Johnny Reb might complain about the boredom of life in camp, but several days on the march would have them writing home with a new set of complaints. "No pen can describe the sufferings and physical exhaustion of an army of infantry marching thirty miles a day," wrote Billy Yank Theodore Gerrish in his memoir. The generals, of course, decided when the army needed to be on the move. And their decisions had to be strategic ones. Obviously, the leaders on both sides wished to order their armies to be on the march only when the weather was good. That way the armies could make the best time in getting to wherever their generals needed them to be. But the weather often didn't cooperate.

These troops of the 6th Maine Infantry posed for a photo during the 1860s before setting out on yet another march.

MARCHING MISERY

Soldiers' accounts aren't clear on what would be considered "good" marching weather. The complaints of Billy Yank and Johnny Reb pretty much cover any kind of conditions on the march. The roads were either too dry. So the dust kicked up by the marching armies would choke them as they trudged along. Or torrential rains occurred. So they would have to slog through knee-deep mud. Confederate cadet Jack Stanard, on the march with the other VMI cadets in 1864, wrote home to his mother about one of those muddy marches. He told her, "The roads were awful *perfect loblolly* [thick with mud] all the way and we had to wade through like *hogs*."

> "The roads were awful *perfect loblolly* [thick with mud] all the way and we had to wade through like *hogs*."
> —Confederate cadet Jack Stanard, 1864

Johnny Reb Carlton McCarthy gives a vivid picture of the misery of marching on dry roads. "The nostrils of the men, filled with dust, became dry and feverish, and even the throat did not escape. The 'grit' was felt between the teeth, and the eyes were rendered almost useless. There was dust in eyes, mouth, ears, and hair." But fellow Confederate soldier John Worsham of Stonewall Jackson's Foot Cavalry—so called because they could march almost as fast as mounted soldiers—dreaded more the rainy marches. He describes the progress of the water through his clothing. He gets so wet that "the storm within him breaks loose, resulting in his cursing the Confederacy, the generals, and everything in the army, including himself!"

The marches were also often long, especially if bad weather had the army running behind schedule. Billy Yank Gerrish wrote of seeing men "limp and reel and stagger as they endeavor to keep up with their regiments. These men were doubtless acquainted with fatigue before they entered the army. . . . But this fearful strain in marching so many miles, in heavy marching order, for successive days, is too much for them. Brave, strong men fall fainting by the wayside."

FURTHER DEPRIVATIONS

At the end of days of marching, even if conditions were good, soldiers on both sides found that often their supply trains hadn't kept up with them. When soldiers were given orders to march, they were told to pack food for a certain number of days. If the march continued longer, their supplies might not catch up with the soldiers. Then the soldiers might run out of food or have to sleep alongside the road without their tents.

A supply train such as this one followed the soldiers on the march. Many times the supplies did not arrive when the soldiers camped for the night.

RAILROADS MOVE THE TROOPS

The 1830s and 1840s had been a period of rapid railroad building across the United States. As a result, the Civil War was sometimes called the first Railroad War. For the first time, armies took advantage of the speed of moving men and materials by rail. The soldiers still slogged through the mud on foot for shorter distances. But troop movements of greater distances could be done by rail. Many soldiers reminisced about the cheering crowds at each railroad station they passed on the way to faraway battles.

Two major Civil War battles were fought at Manassas, Virginia. The place's name at the time—Manassas Junction—helps explain why. The Orange and Alexandria Railroad and the Manassas Gap Railroad crossed at this junction. Control of this critical area meant control of all rail traffic in the Shenandoah Valley, an area hotly contested by both sides throughout the long war. Control of the railroads was a major strategy in the Civil War.

In fact, large numbers of Union troops would chase after one small, independent band of Confederate fighters under the command of John Singleton Mosby, called the Gray Ghost. The Union soldiers were trying to stop the damage Mosby and his band were inflicting on the railroad lines. The men did more than just pull up the rails the trains ran on. That problem could be quickly repaired. The more thorough technique they employed involved burning a pile of the wooden railroad ties that the rails rested on. They used the hot fire to bend the rails out of shape. Such damage required new ties and new rail. This much harder fix slowed down Union troop movements and interfered with the war.

Retreating Confederate soldiers destroyed the Orange and Alexandria Railroad in Manassas in 1862.

Miles

0   100   200   300

— 46 —

Father Corby describes an early march of the Irish Brigade: "In the morning we had placed everything in an army wagon . . . so that we were now left without anything to eat and with nothing to sleep on. . . . But, you may ask, where are the materials that were put into the army wagon? They are there, but the wagons are 'stuck in the mud'—Virginia mud—ten or fifteen miles behind. Next morning we rose from the ground!—to march! No breakfast, and, as we advanced, we left the army wagons still farther behind us."

At times the lack of sleep came not just from lack of shelter. Sometimes the soldiers continued marching well into the night. When finally told to halt, they could not even see well enough to pick out a good location for camp. Union soldier George F. Williams remembered a night when they marched until one in the morning: "Then came the welcome order to lie down and rest. As the column halted in the darkness, the men threw themselves on the narrow strips of sward by the roadside, sleeping in long rows as they lay wrapped in their blankets and ponchos."

There *was* one benefit to being on the march. The soldiers, both Billy Yank and Johnny Reb, felt that much of their time spent in camp was wasted. At least on the march, they were moving. If they were moving, it meant that they were on their way to a battle. Battles had their horrors, but being in battle might mean that the end of the war was closer. So the soldiers welcomed the order to pack rations and prepare for a march. Johnny Reb Carlton McCarthy summed it up this way: "After all, the march had more pleasure than pain."

> " I didn't come out here to fight this way; I wish the earth would crack open and let me drop in."
> —a Confederate soldier from Georgia, 1861

CHAPTER SEVEN

WORDS FROM THE FRONT LINES

Of all the material written by Civil War soldiers, nothing compares with their accounts of the horrors of battle. Their words show us how "seeing the elephant," as they called seeing combat for the first time, changed their lives forever. From the chaotic battle at Manassas in 1861 to the closing scenes near Petersburg, Virginia, in 1865, Billy Yank and Johnny Reb witnessed carnage on a scale that U.S. soldiers had never experienced before.

BATTLE FIRSTHAND

From Manassas, "I remember that my first sensation was one of astonishment at the peculiar whir of the bullets," wrote Elisha Rhodes of the 2nd Rhode Island Regiment. Wrote a Johnny Reb from Georgia: "I didn't come out here to fight this way; I wish the earth would crack open and let me drop in." But Manassas in July 1861

Noted American artist Thure de Thulstrup created this image of the Battle of Shiloh (1862) after the war.

was not the expected one-time battle of the war. It was only the first in a long series of bloody battles that Billy Yank and Johnny Reb would have to fight. The "peculiar whir of the bullets" would become an all-too-familiar sound.

In the spring of 1862, the war began in earnest. Soldiers had committed to serve a three-year term and had trained for months. The first major engagement was in the West, at Shiloh, Tennessee. Hurrying forward to support a Confederate line that was beginning to weaken, Sam Watkins came upon his first sight of battle. "Men were lying in every conceivable position; the dead lying with their eyes wide open, the wounded begging piteously for help. . . . It all seemed to me a dream." A Union soldier enduring the Confederate attack watched in amazement as "a rabbit, trembling with fear, rushes out of the brush in which the rebel battery is hidden and snuggles up close

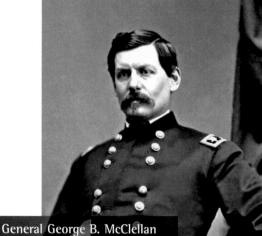

General George B. McClellan and his Union troops were forced to retreat after fighting for two months in a series of battles in 1862 called the Peninsula Campaign.

to a soldier, his natural terror of man entirely subdued by the dreadful surroundings."

In the East, meanwhile, the Army of the Potomac was trying to reach Richmond, Virginia, the Confederate capital. This Union army was under the command of the popular general George B. McClellan. He was trying to take the back route to Richmond, up the peninsula between the York and James rivers. McClellan's army and the Confederate's Army of Northern Virginia fought a series of battles that became known as the Peninsula Campaign. After two months on the peninsula, McClellan's army retreated to its starting point. This would be no rout, as at Manassas, but rather a disciplined retreat under fire. The horror of this retreat stayed in the minds of the participants. Wrote Union soldier George F. Williams: "For seven weary days we fought from early dawn until far into the night.... Battle after battle was fought, until we ceased counting the engagements.... We struggled through swamps, and waded swollen streams.... Amidst a hellish confusion of sounds we fought on ... fighting with the courage born of despair."

LATE IN 1862

The campaigns of 1862 continued with the Johnny Rebs earning most of the honors. The year ended with two of the most horrific battles in U.S. history. The first was fought on September 17 near Sharpsburg,

Maryland, along Antietam Creek. The Battle of Antietam earned itself a dubious honor. On that date, more Americans died or were wounded in battle than on any other day in our history.

The most powerful accounts of this battle describe two fights—one in a cornfield bordered by woods, the other on a small sunken farm road. The cornfield ground was bitterly contested. The Union and Confederate armies together lost about six thousand soldiers there in fighting that at times was hand to hand. As the armies moved back and forth, wounded soldiers who might have been saved were trampled to death or shot yet again. Wrote one Union soldier, Eugene Powell from Ohio, "The sight at the fence, where the enemy was standing when we gave our first fire, was awful beyond description . . . dead men were literally piled upon and across each other."

The fight at the sunken road, which would be forever known as Bloody Lane, was another

Two days after the 1862 battle on a road that became known as Bloody Lane, the sunken road was still littered with the bodies of Confederate soldiers.

story of death. Here, after countless charges by Union troops, including the Irish Brigade's most costly fight of the war, the Confederates were finally defeated. But they were not able to retreat. They died on the road, and the photographs taken several days later of their bodies lying on top of one another shocked the nation.

THE TELEGRAPH AND INSTANT NEWS

As the railroad lines moved across the United States in the 1800s, the telegraph moved with them. By the time the Civil War began, the telegraph was an important communication tool for the military.

President Lincoln was a daily visitor to the War Department's telegraph office. He'd sit for hours as messages brought news from the front lines. This instant communication gave the president and his cabinet (advisers) a unique involvement in the day-to-day decisions of war.

Without the telegraph, the Union army would have been severely limited in many of its operations. This was especially true in Tennessee and Mississippi, where communication with Washington would have to be over such a long distance. With the telegraph, the army fighting far to the west could communicate as effectively as the Army of the Potomac fighting close to Washington, D.C.

Telegraph operators gather while waiting for news.

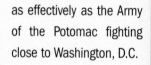

Miles

0   100   200   300

And the year was not over yet. On December 13, 1862, the Union army tried to force the Confederates from a fortified hill near Fredericksburg, Virginia. The Battle of Fredericksburg was a slaughter that went on for two days. Father Corby wrote bitterly that "the place into which Meagher's brigade [The Irish Brigade] was sent was simply a slaughter pen . . . our brigade was cut to pieces." When the fighting stopped, the Union army had been defeated, with 12,700 men dead or wounded. The Confederates won but suffered the loss of 5,300 soldiers.

GETTYSBURG AND OTHER BATTLES

The 1863 campaigns opened with another major Confederate victory at Chancellorsville, Virginia. This gave General Robert E. Lee the confidence to move his troops northward again. They marched into Pennsylvania, where the most important battle of the war—Gettysburg—would take place.

General Lee chose Lieutenant General James Longstreet to coordinate the attack. He picked General George Pickett to lead the charge. When Longstreet ordered the advance, Pickett marched twelve thousand men across one mile of open fields to attack the Union troops on Cemetery Ridge. Amazingly, many of the Johnny Rebs made it to the

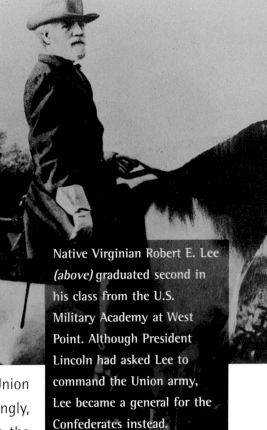

Native Virginian Robert E. Lee (above) graduated second in his class from the U.S. Military Academy at West Point. Although President Lincoln had asked Lee to command the Union army, Lee became a general for the Confederates instead.

enemy positions. The fighting there was hand to hand. Pickett's Charge looked like it might actually succeed. But a group of Vermont regiments helped save the Union army. Wheelock Veazey, commanding the 16th Vermont, led the charge. "With a mighty shout the rush forward was made, and, before the enemy could change his front, we had struck his flank, and swept down the line." As General Pickett's Johnny Rebs retreated back across the field, the Confederacy lost its best chance to end the war on its terms.

The fighting of 1863 continued with major battles on the western front at Chickamauga in Georgia and Chattanooga in Tennessee. The eastern United States remained quiet. But that changed on March 9, 1864. At that time, President Lincoln named General Ulysses S. "Unconditional Surrender" Grant to head the Army of the Potomac. Grant was the hero of Shiloh and Vicksburg. President Lincoln respected him for his determination and his philosophy of continuing to fight even when he suffered setbacks.

> "The incessant roar of the rifle; the screaming bullets; the forest on fire; men cheering, groaning, yelling, swearing and praying! All this created an experience in the minds of the survivors that we can never forget."
>
> —Theodore Gerrish, 1864

During the Battle of the Wilderness in May 1864 in Virginia, soldiers dealt not only with fighting. They also found the rotting bodies of soldiers who had died on the same ground the year before during the Battle of Chancellorsville (May 1863). The Wilderness Campaign was hellish, as the fire of the rifles set the dry underbrush on fire. About two hundred soldiers who could not be moved to safety in

These soldiers were wounded in the Battle of the Wilderness near Fredericksburg, Virginia, in 1864.

time were burned alive. Billy Yank Theodore Gerrish of Maine was there. He remembered "a medley of sounds,—the incessant roar of the rifle; the screaming bullets; the forest on fire; men cheering, groaning, yelling, swearing and praying! All this created an experience in the minds of the survivors that we can never forget." A few days later, Billy Yank and Johnny Reb would again meet at Spotsylvania, Virginia. In front of their position, one of the Johnny Rebs raised a white rag attached to his musket. Accepting this as the traditional sign of a truce, a Vermont soldier stood up to see what they wanted. He was met with a hail of bullets and killed. Union soldier and fellow Vermonter William Noyes was "infuriated beyond control by such treachery and determined upon revenge." He had his fellow soldiers all load their rifles. Then Noyes jumped up on top of the fortifications and began firing down into the Johnny Rebs as fast as he could be handed the loaded rifles. Amazingly, he fired fifteen rifles and was not injured. Trying to explain how he was not all that heroic, he noted that "the enemy did not seem to regain their wits until I had fired five or six shots."

FIGHTING TO THE END

The two armies raced southward. Grant planned to take Petersburg, Virginia. This town was located twenty miles south of the Confederate capital at Richmond. The Johnny Rebs arrived in Petersburg first in June 1864. Both sides began to dig in for a very different kind of war, one that would last ten months. Billy Yank and Johnny Reb lived that time in fortified trenches that stretched from Petersburg to Richmond. They engaged in artillery and sniper warfare with occasional

Union troops lived in the trenches on the outskirts of Petersburg, Virginia, in 1864. These men would eventually find themselves in a bloody forty-five-day standoff with the Confederate army.

attempts to break through the lines. Confederate soldier John Wise found life in the trenches "indescribably monotonous and uncomfortable." He found the heat on sunny days to be intense and rainy days found himself "ankle-deep in tough, clinging mud." With the army trenches only about two hundred yards apart in some places, there was constant danger. Wise noted that because "both sides had attained accurate marksmanship . . . even the act of going to a spring for water involved risk of life or limb."

Johnny Reb and Billy Yank actually became quite friendly at times during the long siege. Either side could call for a truce. Then they would talk or even exchange items. Wise notes that the truce would end "by some one calling out from the rifle-pits that orders had come to reopen fire at a designated time, sufficiently remote to allow everybody to seek cover." And then the war would go on.

Sometimes when the war went on, it was quite spectacular. A Union plan was hatched to undermine the siege works at Petersburg. The soldiers dug tunnels under them and filled the tunnels with explosives. This plan led to a violent explosion that briefly confused the enemy. Then an African American regiment was ordered to charge. The troops marched into their assigned positions. Later, their commander, a white officer named Robert Beecham, made a report. "The Confederates soon recovered from their confusion and concentrated their batteries upon us, catching us like sheep in a slaughter pen."

Beecham was taken prisoner by the end of the battle. The losses to his unit were one-third killed, wounded, or missing. In the years after the war, when critics said that it was the African American regiments that had failed to execute the Union plan, Beecham strongly defended their actions that day. "The [African American] boys formed promptly. There was no flinching on their part. They came [shoulder to shoulder] like true soldiers, as ready to face the enemy and meet death on the field as the bravest and best soldiers that ever lived."

The war also continued in the Deep South. General William Tecumseh Sherman made his historic and devastating march across Georgia and to Atlanta to cut the Confederacy in half. His goal was to stop the resupply of Virginia and its army. In one of the most memorable communications of the Civil War, Union general William T. Sherman sent a telegram to President Abraham Lincoln on December 23, 1864. He told him that he was presenting the city of Savannah, Georgia, to him as a Christmas present.

The Confederate army made several desperate attempts to attack Washington, D.C., mainly to draw off General Grant's troops from the siege at Petersburg. But overall, everyone seemed to know that the end was not far away. Union engineer Thomas Owen wrote home on March 30, 1865. "The rebellion is in its last reel and, within the next few months, will fall prostrate before the victorious armies of the U.S." The end was even closer than this Billy Yank thought.

> " It has been said by comrades who were at that gun as cannoneers that I inserted the shell into the gun after my arm was torn off, before I fell."
>
> —Private John Johnson, 1862

CHAPTER EIGHT

HEROES

"While carrying two case shots to the gun, having cut the fuse of one and made it ready [to] be inserted, I was wounded by a piece of shell, which carried away my right arm at the shoulder, with a portion of the clavicle and scapula. So much of the shoulder was carried away that the cavity of the body was exposed, and the tissue of the lungs made plainly visible. It has been said by comrades who were at that gun as cannoneers that I inserted the shell into the gun after my arm was torn off, before I fell." Private John Johnson, a Billy Yank from Wisconsin, gives this gruesome account of the injury he received at Fredericksburg in 1862, an action that earned him the Congressional Medal of Honor.

DEEDS OF VALOR

About one thousand Billy Yanks earned the Medal of Honor. This award came to Union soldiers who exhibited unusual bravery in battle

THE FIRST WOMAN MEDALIST

Born in New York State, Mary Walker earned her medical degree in 1855. She joined the Union army soon after the war started. At first, the army didn't allow her to work as a doctor, only as a nurse. Eventually, she won an appointment as army surgeon. She worked at field hospitals at some of the Civil War's worst battles, including Chickamauga and Chattanooga. In 1864 the Confederate army captured her and put her in prison. She was exchanged for a Confederate officer soon afterward. In 1866, for her service during the war, she received the Congressional Medal of Honor, the first woman so honored. She wore the medal proudly throughout her lifetime.

Dr. Mary Walker, 1866

conditions. Some years after the end of the Civil War, an effort was made to collect the stories of these medal winners. The resulting book, *Deeds of Valor* (1901), gives a wonderful picture of the heroism of Billy Yank. Included are dozens of stories of soldiers who risked their lives on the battlefield. Many of the stories tell of soldiers who braved enemy fire to rescue wounded friends. Many others tell of soldiers like John Johnson who, after being wounded themselves, continued to offer heroic service.

Peter McAdams, an Irishman and a member of a Pennsylvania unit, begged his captain for the chance to return to the battlefield.

He wanted to bring a wounded soldier to safety behind the lines. When the captain gave permission, he went out onto the field "on a dead run and under heavy fire." As he reached his own lines carrying his friend on his shoulders, he was in for a surprise. "A number of rebel soldiers, perhaps twenty, who witnessed the incident from a position behind the fence, cheered as they observed me escape their fire with my burden and gain the lines of my regiment. Our own men returned the cheer."

Another rescue, which earned Eldridge Robinson of Ohio the Medal of Honor, was much scarier. He and the other soldier involved reached their comrade, Price Worthington,

The Medal of Honor was awarded to Union soldiers for exceptional bravery in battle. It is the highest U.S. military decoration.

who had been shot. Robinson wrote of their attempt to return to their own lines: "We picked him up, and, amid a rain of bullets, of which one hit the wounded man in the leg, and many cut holes in our clothes, we reached the top of the hill, when the gunner or a battery about seventy-five yards in the rear of our line, taking us for the enemy, sent a shell so close to our heads that we were both thrown to the ground."

Private John Chase from Maine rescued himself to earn the Medal of Honor. "One of those shrapnel shells exploded near me and forty-eight pieces of it entered my body. My right arm was shattered and my left eye was put out. I was carried a short distance to the rear as dead, and knew nothing more until two days after. When I regained consciousness, I was in a wagon with a lot of dead comrades being carted to the trenches to be buried. I moaned and called the attention of the driver, who came to my assistance." When Chase finally arrived at the hospital, the doctors told him there was no hope. At one point, the head surgeon told him he had less than six hours to live. But three months later, Private Chase left that hospital to begin his recuperation and return home to Maine.

FEARLESS AND CALM

Several soldiers earned medals for defending the regimental flags that were in their care. Sergeant William H. Carney—a member of the 54th Massachusetts, the famous unit of African American soldiers—protected his flag in spite of enormous danger during the unit's attack on Fort Wagner in South Carolina. He wrote, "In less than twenty minutes I found myself alone struggling upon the ramparts, while all around me lay the dead and wounded piled one upon another. As I could not go into the fort alone, I knelt down, still holding the flag in my hands. The musket balls and grape shot were flying all around me, and as they struck, the sand would fly in my face."

Finally, he decided it was time to retreat and bring the flag to safety. "Upon rising to determine my course to the rear, I was struck by a bullet, but, as I was not prostrated by the shot, I continued my course. I had not gone very far, however, before I was struck by a second ball." A New York soldier had to help him, but Carney was determined to finish his task. "While on our way I was again wounded, this time in the head, and my rescuer then offered to carry the colors for me, but I refused to give them up, saying that no one but a member of my regiment should carry them." Finally arriving at the rear, he was proudest that "the old flag had never touched the ground."

Private Martin Scheibner from Pennsylvania showed that a calm response can save a dangerous situation and earn the Congressional Medal of Honor. A cannon shell landed in the middle of a group of soldiers with its fuse still burning. Everyone else scattered to get away from the shell before it exploded. But Scheibner opened his canteen and poured his coffee on the burning fuse. The report on the incident notes that "the fuse had just about reached the shell" when his calm action saved them all from danger."

Some of the heroic stories are even amusing. Private Delano J.

A print created in 1890 shows the bravery of the 54th Massachusetts, an African American unit of the Union Army, at the Battle of Fort Wagner (1863).

Morey, an Ohio soldier retreating with his company, saw two Confederate sharpshooters. He charged at them alone as they loaded their guns to shoot him. The only problem was that his own gun was not loaded. That didn't stop him. Morey remembers "I was a little too quick for them. I leveled my empty gun at them and ordered them to surrender, which they promptly did, and I led the captives to my captain. I was sixteen years old, and each of my prisoners was old enough to be my father."

> "I was a little too quick for them. I leveled my empty gun at them and ordered them to surrender, which they promptly did, and I led the captives to my captain."
>
> —Private Delano J. Morey, 1862

The stories of these heroic Billy Yanks were saved because they were awarded the Congressional Medal of Honor. No specific book about Johnny Rebs' heroic deeds exists. But no doubt as many heroic efforts occurred among the Confederates as among the Union soldiers. One famous story illustrates the Confederates' valor under fire.

During the horrible Battle of Fredericksburg in 1862, Union troops assaulted Confederates in a secure position behind a stone wall. Many Union soldiers died on the field. But many others who were wounded had to stay on the field until the battle was over. They suffered horribly. Their cries for water caused a Confederate soldier to earn himself the title the Angel of Marye's Heights. South Carolina soldier Richard Kirkland climbed over the wall while Union fire continued. He brought water to the wounded Union soldiers

The Kirkland Monument honors the kindness of Richard Kirkland, a Johnny Reb from South Carolina who gave water to many wounded Billy Yanks after battle.

suffering on the field. A statue near the stone wall honors his courageous actions. He saw the wounded Union soldiers not as enemies but as suffering human beings.

> **"If I remained where I was, the most favorable result that I could hope for was captivity, which, in reality, would be worse . . . ."**
>
> — Theodore Gerrish, 1864

CHAPTER NINE
WOUNDED

"Just as Major Spear received the order to retreat, I was wounded, a minie-ball passing through my left ankle. It is impossible to describe the sensations experienced by a person when wounded for the first time." So wrote Billy Yank Theodore Gerrish during the Battle of the Wilderness. But even worse than being wounded was Gerrish's situation. "Our regiment was rapidly retreating, and the rebels as rapidly advancing. The forest trees around me were on fire, and the bullets were falling thick and fast. If I remained where I was, the most favorable result that I could hope for was captivity, which, in reality, would be worse than death by the bullet on the field."

Gerrish recovered, returned to the 20th Maine, and fought until the end of the war. How he escaped his predicament is a tribute to his determination not to be left behind on the battlefield. He forced himself to his feet and discovered that he could manage to run as long as he kept his leg perfectly straight. "Fear lent wings to my flight, and away I dashed. Frequently my wounded leg would refuse to do good service, and as a result I would tumble headlong upon

— 66 —

the ground, then rising, I would rush on again." Finally, he reached the field hospital. He waited three days to have his wound cared for. Then he was transported to a hospital in a baggage wagon with twelve other soldiers. His memory of that time? "Those were terrible hours. How plainly they are pictured upon my mind!"

THE GREATEST FEAR

Over and over again, accounts speak of the soldiers' greatest fear— being seriously wounded but not killed outright. The stories of soldiers risking their own deaths to bring back their wounded friends reflect that fear. Soldiers knew that to be wounded and left on the battle- field in the care of the enemy was the worst possible fate. Yet, a Confederate officer, William Oates, commander of the 15th Alabama, acknowledged that the wounded soldiers he left at the famous Battle of Gettysburg in 1863 "were as well cared for as any wounded soldiers in the hands of an enemy ever are." This was a grudging statement and only partly a compliment to the Union surgeons. The

Bodies of the dead and wounded littered the battlefields after the fighting stopped. These soldiers died during the second day of fighting at Gettysburg in July 1863.

reality was, after a battle, the victors held possession of the battle-field. They took care of their own wounded first. Then they provided care to their wounded enemy prisoners. But, in a battle such as Gettysburg—where the number of wounded soldiers far exceeded the availability of surgeons—the wait could be several days. In the case of the wounded of the 15th Alabama, two or three days passed before the soldiers were assisted. Oates told of one soldier who lay in the rain for two days. "He lay on his back, could not turn, and kept from drowning by putting his hat over his face." This particular sol-dier survived his ordeal. Many others, desperately needing medical attention, died in the fields before anyone was available to care for them.

Many soldiers died on the battlefield while waiting for medical attention that never arrived. This image is from the 1862 battle at Fredericksburg, Virginia.

BACK TO CAMP, BACK TO WAR

After battle, wounded soldiers who could walk made their way back to field hospitals set up behind the battle lines. Those who could not leave the battlefield without help hoped for friends to return for them. Drummer boys, assigned as stretcher bearers, also came to get them and bring them to field hospitals. Surgeons treated soldiers whom they thought might recover and then had them transported away from the battlefield.

Transport from the battlefield was also a grueling experience. William Reed was involved with the Sanitary Commission that provided care to the soldiers. He described the "privilege" of ambulance transport away from the battlefield. "What a privilege!" he wrote. "A privilege of being violently tossed from side to side, of having one of the four who occupy the vehicle together thrown bodily, perhaps,

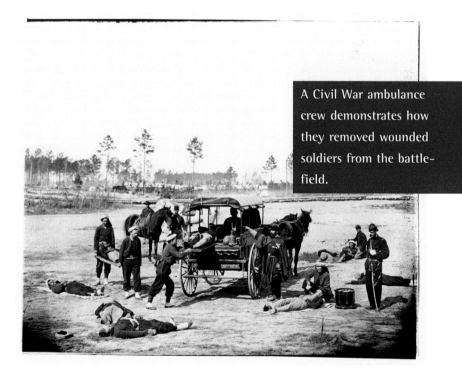

A Civil War ambulance crew demonstrates how they removed wounded soldiers from the battlefield.

upon a gaping wound; of being tortured, and racked, and jolted, when each jarring of the ambulance is enough to make the sympathetic brain burst with agony."

As the war progressed, soldiers who made it off the battlefield and back to the general hospitals usually survived their injuries. Hospitals had improved, and their staffs had learned more about what care would bring the best results. But three out of every four surgeries were amputations. Survival involved long months of rehabilitation. The victim had to learn how to cope with an artificial limb and try to get back to living a normal life.

Some soldiers had minor wounds. They returned to their units to fight after they had recovered. Many Union soldiers who had moderately serious wounds but were no longer fit to fight also remained in the army. They served in the Veteran Reserve Corps that was founded in 1863. They were guards, prisoner escorts, nurses, and cooks.

Women helped care for patients at Carver General Hospital in Washington, D.C., during the Civil War.

THE RIFLE THAT REVOLUTIONIZED MEDICINE

Warfare encourages advances in military weaponry. However, it also encourages advances in medicine to attempt to repair the different kinds of damage being caused by the new weapons. The rifle used by soldiers in the Civil War illustrates this cycle.

In the American Revolution (1775–1783), many soldiers used smoothbore muskets that fired round lead balls. The muskets had a fairly limited range. From a tactical perspective, they didn't do enough damage when they actually hit someone. The ball tended to stop when it impacted with bone. A more effective weapon was needed.

The rifled musket was the answer. The Springfield was the most common type used in the Civil War. The inside of the gun barrel was rifled with a spiral groove. A cone-shaped bullet was created with matching grooves, which could make it spin up the barrel. When fired, it had more distance and power. Being more powerful on impact meant that it would drive through clothing, skin, tissue, and muscle into the bone, usually fracturing it. Such an injury would do much more damage. Often surgeons had to amputate a limb to save the soldier from infection. Most soldiers on both sides began the war with smoothbore muskets. But by the end of the conflict, just about everyone was using the new rifled muskets.

Doctors in the Civil War found themselves confronted with horrible wounds and the resulting piles of amputated arms and legs. Eventually, they devised a new medical procedure, called resection, that attempted to save the limbs of injured soldiers. The technique was not always successful. The best results happened when the limb could be immobilized. This need for immobilization led to the invention of splints. Those who benefited from the surgery saved their arm or leg. The need to create a more powerful weapon had again led to a corresponding breakthrough in medicine.

Soldiers of the Veteran Reserve Corps stationed in Alexandria, Virginia

Alfred Bellard of New Jersey was wounded in the leg at the Battle of Chancellorsville in May 1863. His injury did not require amputation, but he was not considered recovered until October. He was reassigned to the Veteran Reserve Corps. Bellard spent the rest of the war with the Corps. He even had a chance to be a hero.

In July 1864, Confederate general Jubal Early snuck up the Shenandoah Valley into Maryland. He made a surprise attack on Fort Stevens outside of Washington, D.C. The Veteran Reserve Corps held off the Confederate troops until reinforcements arrived from Grant's army in Virginia. They received a hero's welcome from the residents of Washington. Bellard noted that the residents "were glad to see the Regt. [regiment] back again as they were well thought of for their efficiency and soldierly bearing."

> "The floors, walls, clothes, and the bodies of the men swarm with vermin."
>
> —anonymous Union soldier imprisoned at Libby Prison in Richmond, 1862

CHAPTER TEN

PRISONER OF WAR

A wounded soldier who was behind enemy lines became a prisoner of war (POW). Many soldiers found this option about as horrible as being left for dead. After being wounded, Theodore Gerrish said, "If I remained where I was the most favorable result that I could hope for was captivity, which, in reality, would be worse than death."

Billy Yanks dreaded the thought of being imprisoned at places such as Andersonville, Georgia, where thirteen thousand Union soldiers died. The Confederate Libby Prison in Richmond was no better. "The floors, walls, clothes, and the bodies of the men swarm with vermin," said one Union soldier imprisoned there for several weeks. Likewise, Johnny Reb feared the Union prisons. The one advantage that Johnny Reb had in being a Union POW was that the food was better and more readily available. As conditions in the South worsened, Billy Yanks in prison faced starvation.

The life of the soldiers held as prisoners was truly horrible. But

Union troops commented that they would rather die than be held captive at Libby Prison in Richmond, Virginia.

as one historian put it, "Unpleasant as is the story of the prisons of the Civil War, however great their shortcomings, the treatment of prisoners...marks a decided advance over the general practice of the world before that time."

BY THE RULES

Rules existed during the Civil War—and still exist in modern times—about how POWs are to be treated. They have to be protected from harm and given a place to live. They are to be provided with food, clothing, and medical care if they need it. They are to be supplied with other basic necessities, such as bedding and fuel, to keep them alive and reasonably well. Nations worldwide have agreed upon these rules. Unfortunately, during war, when such rules are most needed, they are sometimes not followed.

The Civil War was even more complicated. It wasn't a war between two countries but a fight to keep one country together. Early on, the Union tried to claim that prisoners taken in battle were not POWs at all. Instead, they were people who had committed treason against their country and should be killed. The Confederacy reacted by threatening to treat Billy Yanks the same way and kill them. Finally, both sides agreed to follow the normal POW rules.

The first problem both sides had was to find enough places to house all the prisoners who were being taken in battle. Historians still argue over how many Civil War soldiers were POWs. One report says that about 211,000 Billy Yanks and 460,000 Johnny Rebs were taken prisoner during the conflict.

The other serious problem was finding enough food and supplies to provide for them. Both governments were already struggling to find enough room and supplies for their own armies. The Union and Confederate governments issued orders that their prisoners would be treated as well as their own soldiers. They would receive the same rations as regular soldiers and the same supplies. While these were the standards set for treating prisoners, POW conditions were usually far worse.

POW CONDITIONS

The Confederate prison at Andersonville, Georgia, is remembered as the most horrible of all the camps on either side. This camp was built to hold ten thousand soldiers. At one point, in August 1864, thirty-three hundred Union soldiers were housed there. The prisoners were not allowed to build shelters because there was not enough room. They lived in holes they dug in the ground with their hands. Rations were scarce. According to one account, the POWs had "a teaspoon of salt, three tablespoons of beans, and half a pint of unsifted cornmeal." Even Southerners felt pity for the conditions the Union soldiers at Andersonville had to endure. Wrote one Southern woman, "My heart aches for these poor wretches, Yankees though they are, and I am afraid God will suffer some terrible retribution to fall upon us for letting such things happen."

If Andersonville was the worst, the experiences of soldiers at other prison camps were not much better. Union colonel John Coburn filed this official report on the treatment of his troops taken prisoner in Tennessee: "The men, shivering, half-starved, without

Andersonville Prison in Georgia was considered one of the most horrible camps on either side. This is the view from the main gate, where prisoners were awaiting their ration of food.

sleep or rest, were then crowded into box-cars. . . . The floor of the one I was in was covered with wet manure. Thus we traveled that day to Chattanooga. On arriving there, we were placed, without rations, for the night in a large frame house just erected for a hospital; crowded in, almost to suffocation."

Colonel Coburn was eventually transferred to Libby Prison in Richmond, Virginia. He described their food as "half a pound a day of bread and of putrid, starveling meat, totally unfit for use, filling the room with a foul stench on being brought in." Another Union prisoner confined at Libby Prison spoke of the terrible conditions there, "I sincerely hope that rebel officers in our hands will be compelled to live on similar short allowances."

Similar complaints were reported about conditions in the Union's prisons. The secretary of state wrote to the secretary of war after a British diplomat filed a complaint. The diplomat was offended by the conditions of Confederate prisoners at Fort Delaware. The prison's walls were described as "wet with moisture, the stone floor damp and cold, the air impure and deathly, no bed or couches to lie upon and offensive vermin crawling in every direction."

PRISON DEATH TOLLS

Historians not only disagree about how many Union and Confederate soldiers were POWs. They also disagree about how many of them died in captivity. The best estimates are that thirty thousand Billy Yanks and twenty-six thousand Johnny Rebs died while in prison. A prisoner exchange program existed between the North and the South. But it worked less effectively as the war continued. One major problem occurred once African American Union troops become POWs. President Jefferson Davis ordered that African American prisoners be treated as "slaves in insurrection." Many were executed on the spot. Three hundred African American POWs were shot after the 1864 battle at Fort Pillow in Tennessee. Others were sold as slaves.

Hannah Johnson, the mother of a soldier in the 54th Massachusetts, wrote directly to Abraham Lincoln. She was concerned about the treatment of African American prisoners, even though her son had not been taken prisoner. "I know that a colored man ought to run no greater risques [risks] than a white, his pay is no greater his obligation to fight is the same. So why should not our enemies be compelled to treat him the same.... Now Mr Lincoln dont you think you [ought] to stop this thing and make them do the same by the colored men.... We poor oppressed ones appeal to you, and ask fair play." General Grant ordered that no prisoner exchanges

A great number of soldiers died while in captivity. At Andersonville Prison, mass burials filled large trenches.

would occur again until the South treated African American prisoners equally. The South refused, and the prisoner exchange program ended.

The gruesome conditions and the very real risk of dying while being a POW prompted many soldiers to try to escape. One famous escape from Libby Prison occurred in February 1864. By then Libby Prison housed only Union officers, and they were carefully watched. Yet 109 of them still managed a spectacular escape by crawling through a tunnel that they dug under the wall of the prison and that came out across the street. More would have escaped except that they became too loud and their noise brought the guards. The Confederates recaptured 48, and 2 drowned. But the rest made it to the Union lines. As word spread about horrible prison conditions, many soldiers saw being captured as being worse than death.

grave. All the while, you realized it could just as easily have been you who had been killed in the battle.

Many soldiers' accounts speak of the deaths of friends who had a feeling before the battle that they would die. Union soldier William Lord described finding his friend, Private Reed, dead on the battlefield in 1864. "Only the night before Reed told me that he felt as if he would be killed soon. 'If I am, Bill,' said he, 'go through my pockets and send the few belongings I have to my family.' There he was, poor fellow—dead! I stopped long enough to carry out his request."

Elisha Rhodes of the 2nd Rhode Island tells of a soldier who "showed me a board on which he had carved his name, date of birth and had left a place for his date of death.... I asked him if he expected to be

This is the kind of scene that many soldiers had to deal with while tending to the dead bodies of fellow soldiers after battle. This image was taken after the Battle of Antietam in 1862.

Statistics about the Civil War

Population of the United States (1860s):
   34,300,000 (Union: 26,200,000; Confederacy: 8,100,000)

Number of soldiers:
   3,867,500 (Union: 2,803,300; Confederacy: 1,064,200)

Percentage of participation:
   11.1% (Union: 10.7%; Confederacy: 13.1%)

Deaths in combat:
   184,594 (Union: 110,070; Confederacy: 74,524)

Other soldier deaths (disease, accident, etc.):
   373,458 (Union: 249,458; Confederacy: 124,000)

Wounded:
   412,175 (Union: 275,175; Confederacy: 137,000).
   The exact numbers are unknown.

Death rate: 1.7%

Overall casualty rate: 25.1%

Source: U.S. Department of Defense

killed and he said no, and that he had made his head board only for fun." The soldier was killed in the fighting near Petersburg, Virginia, the next day.

John Wise, a VMI cadet who gained fame at the Battle of New Market, Virginia, in 1864 wrote later about his roommate, Jack

Stanard. Jack had "con-fessed a presentiment that he would be killed" the night before the battle. Both cadets had been ordered to stay behind and guard the supply wagons. But they decided together to disobey their orders and join the battle. Afterward, John Wise felt guilty "for my part in drawing him into the fight." When it ended, he went searching for his roommate. But he was too late: "Stanard had breathed his last but a few moments

Two Confederate friends posed before leaving for battle in 1862.

before we reached the old farmhouse.... His body was still warm." Wise, seventeen years old and wounded, was left with the task of writing to Stanard's mother. He told her that her son had "died at this post fighting gallantly for his country's cause."

WRITING HOME

Perhaps what made dealing with death so real was that it was so commonplace. Most regiments were formed from local communi-ties. So Billy Yank and Johnny Reb were usually fighting with their neighbors by their sides. After a battle, they were often the first bearers of bad tidings. They were the ones who delivered the last messages home, who told how the soldier had died, and gave what comfort they could. The letters written by individuals over the course of the war show the constant litany of deaths.

One of the best descriptions of what made soldiers able to deal with death comes from Carleton McCarthy. "The dangers of the battle-field, and the demands upon his energy, strength, and courage, not only strengthen the old, but almost create new, faculties of mind and heart," he wrote. "The death, sudden and terrible, of those dear to him, the imperative necessity of standing to his duty while the wounded cry and groan ... the terrible thirst, hunger, heat, and weariness—all these teach a boy self-denial, attachment to duty ... and, instead of hardening him, ... make him pity and love even the enemy of his country, who bleeds and dies for *his* country."

> "How they straggled, and how demoralized they seemed!"
>
> —John Wise, 1865

CHAPTER TWELVE

FINALLY, THE END

Sunday, April 2, 1865, was "a perfect Sunday of the Southern spring." These were the words of Richmond socialite Constance Cary Harrison. While attending church, she saw a note handed to Confederate president Jefferson Davis. "I happened to sit in the rear of the President's pew," she wrote, "so near that I plainly saw the sort of gray pallor that came upon his face as he read." The note, from General Robert E. Lee, said that the Petersburg siege was about to end. The Confederate army could no longer defend the Confederate capital at Richmond.

As the government pulled out of the capital, chaos erupted. Confederate general Ewell decided to burn the supplies left in the city so they would not fall into Union hands. No one expected the disaster that resulted. LaSalle Pickett, wife of Confederate general George Pickett, was in Richmond on that fateful night. She remembered: "A breeze springing up suddenly from the south fanned the slowly flickering flames into a blaze . . . they were carried to the next building, and the next. . . . Still the flames raged on. They leaped from house to house in mad revel."

CHASING JOHNNY REB

On the morning of April 3, 1865, Union soldiers marched into Richmond. They replaced the Confederate flag flying over the state capitol with the Stars and Stripes. Billy Yanks had spent the last four years trying to march into Richmond. At last, they were there. Abraham Lincoln visited the city the next day. He walked the

Richmond, Virginia, was in ruins after a massive fire set by a Confederate general unexpectedly destroyed the city in 1865.

streets to the Confederate White House and sat at Jefferson Davis's desk. Everyone knew that the war would be over soon.

Only some of the Billy Yanks had the honor of occupying Richmond. Most of them, after the long siege of Petersburg, were on the march again. They were chasing after the Johnny Rebs of the Army of Northern Virginia, hoping for one final confrontation. General Lee had split his retreating army into two sections. He'd ordered both sections to march to the town of Amelia, about thirty-five miles away. Supplies were waiting for them. Confederate lieutenant John Wise was delivering a message to General Lee. He came upon the main body of the retreating Confederates. He wrote: "How they straggled, and how demoralized they seemed!"

General Grant's objective was to stop Lee's army from reaching their supplies. But the Billy Yanks could not stop the rebels before they reached Amelia. In the end, it didn't matter. Instead of food, only ammunition had arrived. By then the Johnny Rebs were starving. Ammunition was not what General Lee needed to keep his army on the march. Johnny Reb Carlton McCarthy records that all that was left was the "corn on the cob intended for the horses. Two ears were issued to each man. It was parched in the coals, mixed with salt, stored in the pockets, and eaten on the road. Chewing the corn was hard work. . . . It made the jaw ache and the gums and the teeth so sore as to cause almost unendurable pain." But that was all the food they would get.

The Billy Yanks sensed that the end was near. They were overjoyed. Dr. Alfred Woodhull remembered: "We were like so many schoolboys on a holiday . . . the spirit of prophecy within us announced that the day of retribution for the wicked Rebels was at hand, that we were surely crushing the rebellion."

But the end was not quite yet. More Billy Yanks and Johnny Rebs would die when the armies met at Sayler's Creek on April 6. The fighting began with small skirmishes. For Carlton McCarthy, it was an exhausting final battle. "The race to the top of the long hill was exceedingly trying to men already exhausted by continual marching, hunger, thirst, and loss of sleep. They ran, panting for breath, like chased animals, fairly staggering as they went." The Union army captured most of the Army of Northern Virginia at the Battle of Sayler's Creek. When the battle was over, the remainder of the Confederate army continued its retreat. They marched toward the small town of Appomattox, Virginia.

General Grant had begun a correspondence with General Lee during the retreat. He wrote to him on April 7: "The results of the last week must convince you of the hopelessness of further resistance." He wanted to end the "further [loss] of blood" and asked Lee to surrender.

"Peace being my great desire, there is but one condition I would insist upon, namely, that the men and officers surrendered shall be disqualified for taking up arms again."

—Union general Ulysses S. Grant, 1865

Lee replied the next day, declining to surrender. Instead, he asked what terms of surrender Grant would be willing to offer. Grant's answering letter was generous and sympathetic, with no hint of a gloating victor. "Peace being my great desire, there is but one condition I would insist upon, namely, that the men and officers surrendered shall be disqualified for taking up arms again."

Surrender at Appomattox

On Sunday, April 9, 1865, General Grant and General Lee met in the parlor of the home of Wilmer McLean in Appomattox Court House. The next day, General Lee sent his General Order No. 9. It ordered the Johnny Rebs to "return to their homes," assuring them of his "unceasing admiration of your constancy and devotion to your country." More important for the starving Confederates was their first meal as a defeated army. Carlton McCarthy wrote: "A line of men came single file over the hill

Union soldiers gathered at Appomattox Court House in Virginia, where Confederate general Lee surrendered to Union general Grant in 1865.

near the camp, each bearing on his shoulder a box of 'hard-tack' or crackers. Behind these came a beef, driven by soldiers. The crackers and beef were a present from the Federal [Union] troops near, who, knowing the famished condition of the surrounded army, had contributed their day's rations for its relief."

Billy Yank Theodore Gerrish was also at Appomattox. He wrote of his feelings toward the defeated enemy: "All of our associations with the rebels at Appomattox were of the most pleasant character. Great care was taken by our soldiers not to wound their feelings, and they exhibited their gratitude by many pleasant words. . . . They had lost all by the war, but they accepted the situation gracefully."

Three days later, on April 12, 1865, the formal "passing of the armies" took place. The Confederate soldiers passed in review. They stacked their arms and turned in their flags. It was a difficult moment for both sides. The Johnny Rebs were admitting defeat after four long years of war. The Billy Yanks also had a difficult job. The ex-Confederate soldiers were their fellow citizens, who were being welcomed back into their country. Gloating had no place in the passing of the armies.

General Grant appointed General Joshua Lawrence Chamberlain to conduct the passing of the armies. The two men shared the view that the moment should be solemn and respectful. They wanted Union soldiers to recognize the courage of the defeated Confederates. So Chamberlain ordered silence as the defeated troops passed by. Then he had the Union soldiers salute their former enemy. Theodore Gerrish remembered: "Our commander, with the true courtesy of a chivalrous spirit, gave the command 'Shoulder arms,' and we thus saluted our fallen enemies. They returned the salute." It was a moment of reconciliation for Johnny Reb and Billy Yank.

General Robert E. Lee *(seated, center)* surrenders to Union general Ulysses S. Grant *(seated, right)* on April 9, 1865.

A touching and significant moment took place at the actual signing of the surrender by General Lee. Lieutenant Colonel Ely Parker, a Seneca Indian from New York, was on hand. He was a member of General Grant's staff and was introduced to General Lee by General Grant. General Lee commented "I am glad to see one real American." Parker answered, "We are all Americans." Indeed, with the war over, we finally were.

> "We gather . . . to sing the old patriotic songs once more."
>
> —Theodore Gerrish, 1882

CHAPTER THIRTEEN

CHANGED FOREVER

With the war over, Billy Yank and Johnny Reb returned to their lives at home. But in some ways, they never left the war behind them. Of course, going home was a very different experience for Johnny Reb than it was for Billy Yank. Following the surrender, the Johnny Rebs headed for home, not knowing what they would find. Most of the fighting had taken place in Southern territory. The first work of most of the Johnny Rebs would be the rebuilding of their homes and communities.

POSTWAR REACTIONS

Carlton McCarthy and a friend headed for Richmond. They had heard that "some young confederates, who were smart, were at work in the ruins cleaning bricks at five dollars a day. Others had government work, as clerks, mechanics, and laborers, earning from one to five dollars a day." They would be required to take a loyalty oath to the U.S. government before they could get a job.

For the most part, the Johnny Rebs accepted that the war was over. They had lost but had fought long and hard. Many of the ex-officers of the Confederate army continued debating the war for the rest their lives. The common Johnny Rebs were more than willing to go on with their lives.

Billy Yank received a hero's welcome at the end of the war. On May 23 and 24, 1865, 150,000 soldiers of the Union army marched in the Grand Review of the Armies in Washington, D.C. Theodore Gerrish felt that the review "reminded us of the histories we had studied in our school days, about the armies of Rome marching in grand procession and carrying the sacred eagles through the Eternal City." He was pleased to have the chance to "march through the streets of the capital of the great Western Republic, amid scenes as magnificent and with steps as haughty, as

The Grand Review of the Armies, a military parade, took place on Pennsylvania Avenue in Washington, D.C., after the war ended. After the parade, the soldiers were sent home.

those of the old Roman soldiers in the days of their pride and power."

After the Grand Review, the various units went back to their home states to be mustered out (discharged from service). Returning home, they didn't have to face a devastated landscape as did the Johnny Rebs. Most had left their homes as young boys. They came back as men. They married their sweethearts and tried to lead normal lives. But they did face a changed world. In many ways, the war stayed with them.

COPING AFTERWARD

The Civil War brought with it great technological change. Weapons had improved. So had the practice of medicine, as doctors found new ways of treating wounded or sick soldiers. But the Civil War also brought with it societal changes, mostly in the role of women. During the Civil War, wives had been left at home. They not only raised the children but also ran the family farms. In addition, women had cared for sick and wounded soldiers. Many of these women had no wish to return to the ways of the past. They liked the independence that the war had forced on them, and they intended to keep it. Soon they used that new independence to try to give themselves a larger role in society.

Many of the soldiers who returned home had injuries that did not allow them to perform their prewar jobs. Three-quarters of the injuries during the Civil War had resulted in amputation. For these soldiers, their wounds would change the plans they had to return home and pick up where they had left off.

Many of the soldiers would never have traveled more than a few miles from their home if they had not gone off to war. They found that they wished to see more of the world. The restlessness of the returning soldiers fueled expansion and helped to populate the vast lands in the western United States.

No matter where they went, both Billy Yank and Johnny Reb kept the memory of the Civil War alive. Rutherford B. Hayes served in the Civil War with the 23rd Ohio Infantry. He later was elected president of the United States. Being elected president usually would be the high point of anyone's career. But for Hayes, his experience in what he called "the glorious war" was the memory that he most treasured. Right up to the end of his life, he would maintain that "the war years were the best years of our lives."

Johnny Reb Carlton McCarthy had a similar view. He noted "no country likes to part with a good earnest war. It likes to talk about the war, write its history, fight its battles over and over again, and build monument after monument to commemorate its glories." Billy Yank Theodore Gerrish felt the same way: "We gather in our Grand Army Halls, to fight our battles over again, to sing the old patriotic songs once more, and under that inspiration, to reform our ranks. . . . We derive satisfaction from that."

WAYS OF REMEMBERING

Billy Yanks organized themselves into groups to remember their glorious past. These groups included the Grand Army of the Republic and the Military Order of the Loyal Legion of the United States. For their male children, there was the Sons of Union Veterans. Johnny Rebs had the United Confederate Veterans and countless other organizations. For women of the South, there was the Daughters of the Confederacy. The soldiers wrote articles for publications such as the *Confederate Veteran*. They visited the sites of their battles.

In July 1913, more than 53,000 Billy Yanks and Johnny Rebs returned to the site of the Battle of Gettysburg. On July 3, soldiers from both sides who had participated in Pickett's Charge faced one another on the same ground. One observer of the reenactment wrote of the excitement as the waiting Billy Yanks scrambled across the wall to meet their oncoming foes. "The emotion of the moment was so contagious that there was scarcely a dry eye in the huge throng." Amazingly, in 1938, more than 1,800 Billy Yanks and Johnny Rebs returned to celebrate the seventy-fifth anniversary of the battle. Most of the men were in their nineties. Some were even over one hundred years old. Although the war was seventy-five years in the past, what lingered was not the horror of the battles that had divided them but rather the shared experience that united them.

Since the Civil War ended so many years ago, many would think we could only read about it in history books. In fact, thousands of people routinely spend their weekends reenacting the lives of Billy Yank and Johnny Reb. They carefully search for any detail that will make the experience more real. Sometimes a reenactor might speak excitedly about finding new information giving detailed instructions

A veteran of the Union army shakes hands with a veteran of the Confederate army during the reunion at Gettysburg, Pennsylvania, in 1913.

Reenactors participate in the annual Civil War battle reenactment at Gettysburg in 2005.

on the correct placement of uniform badges. The reenactors wear the same scratchy wool uniforms, eat the same food, and live as closely as possible under the same conditions as the Civil War soldiers. In the words of Civil War historian and veteran reenactor Brian Pohanka: "As one who has been involved in Civil War living history for twenty years, I have found it a great learning experience. When I read soldiers' accounts I can now apply some sense of what they are describing in the way of drill, tactics, the smell of gunpowder, the heft of musket and knapsack, the cold nights or hot days, the campfire and welcome tin cup of coffee, the camaraderie of my 'pards'... it is a way to bridge the centuries...."

In staging reenactments, these modern Billy Yanks and Johnny Rebs keep the Civil War alive for all of us. They show us how the soldiers lived, how their weapons fired, and what their daily lives were

THE REENACTORS WHO SAVE THE BATTLEFIELDS

Reenactors re-create a variety of periods in history, such as the time of Roman soldiers, or of knights in mock tournaments, or of colonial militiamen during the American Revolution. However, the most numerous reenactments are from the Civil War.

The Civil War, more than any other conflict in U.S. history, seems to have been romanticized. Perhaps because of this, many people spend their weekends living in their own version of that past. As many as twenty thousand reenactors have participated in a single event. Some estimate that more than twenty-five thousand participate regularly, and thousands of others do so occasionally.

Many of the reenactors take that living history one step further. They fight to preserve the land on which the Civil War was fought. Reenactors will often appear as part of fund-raising efforts to preserve battlefield lands. They sometimes raise tens of thousands of dollars to be used to purchase land threatened by modern development. Organizations such as the Civil War Preservation Trust know that they can turn to reenactors to be partners in the shared goal of keeping Civil War history alive. Their shared goal is to give future generations the chance to walk the places where so many Americans, Union and Confederate, fought and died.

like. But the reenactors cannot capture the confusion of battle. They cannot see, smell, and hear the actual horrors that Billy Yank and Johnny Reb experienced.

Every Billy Yank and every Johnny Reb is long dead. But something of their story seems to call to us. And as long as it does, they will never die. Theodore Gerrish knew it would be so: "The country will always honor our memory, and not forget us when we have vanished from its sight. Our graves will not be neglected when there are no Grand Army comrades to scatter their floral offerings upon them."

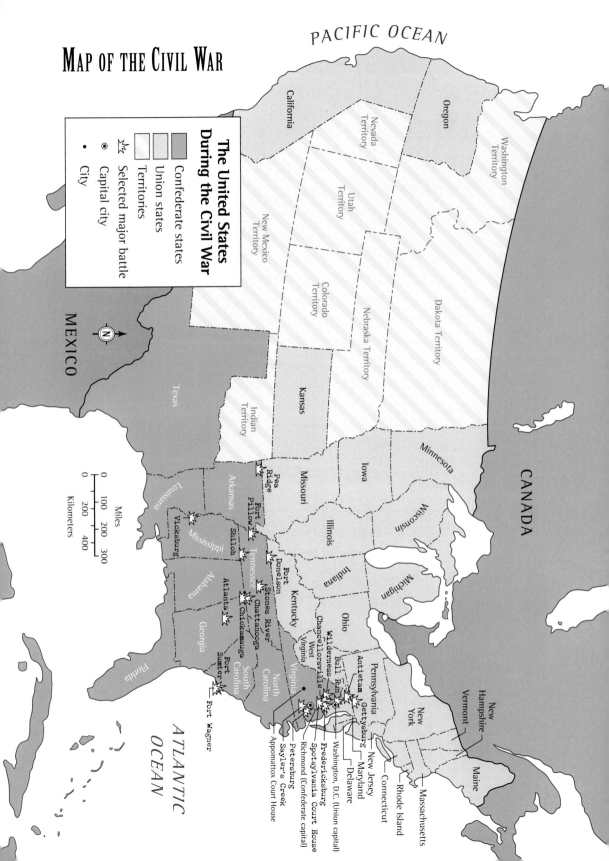

MAP OF THE CIVIL WAR

PACIFIC OCEAN

The United States During the Civil War

Confederate states
Union states
Territories

⚔ Selected major battle
⊗ Capital city
• City

MEXICO

N

CANADA

Washington Territory

Oregon

California

Nevada Territory

Utah Territory

New Mexico Territory

Colorado Territory

Nebraska Territory

Dakota Territory

Kansas

Indian Territory

Texas

Minnesota

Iowa

Missouri

Wisconsin

Illinois

Michigan

Indiana

Ohio

Arkansas

Louisiana

Mississippi

Alabama

Georgia

Tennessee

Kentucky

West Virginia

Virginia

North Carolina

South Carolina

Florida

Pennsylvania

New York

New Jersey

Delaware

Maryland

Vermont

New Hampshire

Maine

Massachusetts

Rhode Island

Connecticut

Pea Ridge

Fort Pillow

Vicksburg

Shiloh

Fort Donelson

Atlanta

Chattanooga

Chickamauga

Stones River

Fort Sumter

Fort Wagner

Wilderness

Chancellorsville

Bull Run

Antietam

Gettysburg

Washington, D.C. (Union capital)

Fredericksburg

Spotsylvania Court House

Richmond (Confederate capital)

Petersburg

Sayler's Creek

Appomattox Court House

Miles
0 100 200
Kilometers
0 200 400
100   300

ATLANTIC OCEAN

Selected Chronology of the Civil War

November 6, 1860	Abraham Lincoln is elected president of the United States.
December 20, 1860	South Carolina secedes from the Union.
February 18, 1861	Jefferson Davis is inaugurated as president of the Confederate States of America.
March 4, 1861	Abraham Lincoln is inaugurated as president of the United States of America.
April 12, 1861	Southern cannons fire on Fort Sumter and the conflict begins.
April 19, 1861	President Lincoln orders a blockade of Southern ports.
May 21, 1861	Richmond, Virginia, is chosen as the capital of the Confederacy.
July 21, 1861	First Battle of Bull Run
February 16, 1862	Fort Donelson falls to Union troops.
April 6–7, 1862	Battle of Shiloh
May–July 1862	Peninsula Campaign, ending with the Seven Days Battle
August 29–30, 1862	Second Battle of Bull Run
September 17, 1862	Battle of Antietam
December 13, 1862	Battle of Fredericksburg
December 31, 1862–January 2, 1863	Battle of Stones River
January 1, 1863	The Emancipation Proclamation takes effect, freeing Confederate slaves.
May 1–4, 1863	Battle of Chancellorsville
July 1–3, 1863	Battle of Gettysburg
July 4, 1863	The siege of Vicksburg, Mississippi, ends with surrender of Confederates.

July 18, 1863	Battle of Fort Wagner
September 19–20, 1863	Battle of Chickamauga
November 19, 1863	President Lincoln delivers the Gettysburg Address.
November 23–25, 1863	Battle of Chattanooga
May 5–6, 1864	Battle of the Wilderness
May 8–19, 1864	Battle of Spotsylvania
June 20, 1864–April 2, 1865	Siege of Petersburg
September 2, 1864	The Union captures Atlanta, Georgia.
November–December 1864	Sherman's March to the Sea
April 3, 1865	Union troops enter the Confederate capital at Richmond.
April 9, 1865	General Lee surrenders to General Grant at Appomattox Court House.
April 14, 1865	Abraham Lincoln is assassinated at Ford's Theatre in Washington, D.C.

Source Notes

6 George Barton, letter of May 19, 1864, quoted in Warren Wilkinson, *Mother, May You Never See the Sights I Have Seen* (New York: William Morrow, 1990), 121.

6–7 Ibid.

8 Theodore Gerrish, *Army Life: A Private's Reminiscences of the Civil War* (Portland, ME: Hoyt, Fogg & Donham, 1882), 15.

8 Carlton McCarthy, *Detailed Minutiae of Soldier Life in the Army of Northern Virginia, 1861–1865* (Richmond: Carlton McCarthy and Company, 1882), 9.

9 Bell Irvin Wiley, *The Life of Billy Yank* (New York: Doubleday & Company, 1952), 299.

11 Geoffrey C. Ward, *The Civil War* (New York: Alfred A. Knopf, 1990), 248.

13 Ibid., 253.

14 Thomas B. Allen, *The Blue and the Gray* (Washington, DC: National Geographic Society, 1992), 167.

15 U.S. War Department, *War of the Rebellion: A Compilation of the Official Records of the Union and Confederate Armies* (Washington, DC: Government Printing Office, 1890–1901), 1st ser., 27:378.

15 Sarah Rosetta Wakeman, *An Uncommon Soldier* (New York: Oxford University Press, 1994), 28, 44.

15 Ibid.

16–17 Gerrish, 15.

17 McCarthy, 193.

18 Gerrish, 19.

18 Oliver W. Norton, *Army Letters 1861–1865* (Chicago: O. L. Deming, 1903), 28.

19 Gerrish, 19.

20 Stephen B. Oates, *With Malice Toward None* (New York: New American Library, 1977), 271.

21 John Macdonald, *Great Battles of the Civil War* (New York: Collier Books, 1988), 12.

21 U.S. War Department, 1st ser., 2:316.

21 Henry N. Blake, "Bull Run: A Union Soldier," in Don Congdon, *Combat: The Civil War* (New York: Mallard Press, 1967), 27.

23 John W. Haley, *The Rebel Yell & the Yankee Hurrah* (Camden, ME: Down East Books, 1985), 28.

23 McCarthy, 29.

23 Gerrish, 45.

24 Ibid.

24 McCarthy, 39.

24 Gerrish, 45.

25 Dale E. Floyd, *The Letters and Diary of Thomas James Owen, Fiftieth New York Volunteer Engineer Regiment, during the Civil War* (Washington, DC: U.S. Government Printing Office, 1985), 5.

25 McCarthy, 31.

26 Floyd, 5.

26 Ibid., 19

26–27 Ibid., 22.

27 McCarthy, 80–81.

28 Ibid., 86.

28 Peter Welsh, *Irish Green and Union Blue* (New York: Fordham University Press, 1986), 41.

28 McCarthy, 92.

29 Gerrish, 136.

31 Elisha Hunt Rhodes, *All for the Union* (New York: Orion Books, 1985), 218.

31 Welsh, 33.

31 Gerrish, 68.

31 Ira Berlin, ed., *Freedom's Soldiers: The Black Military Experience in the Civil War* (Cambridge: Cambridge University Press, 1998), 117.

32 William Bircher, *A Drummer-Boy's Diary: Comprising Four Years of Service with the Second Regiment Minnesota Veteran Volunteers, 1861–1865* (Saint Paul: St. Paul Book and Stationery Company, 1889), 73.

32 Alfred Bellard, *Gone for a Soldier* (Boston: Little, Brown and Company, 1975), 118.

32 McCarthy, 56.

34 Bircher, 73.

35 Arthur W. Bergeron Jr., *The Civil War Reminiscences of Major Silas T. Grisamore, C.S.A.* (Baton Rouge: Louisiana State University Press, 1993), 66.

36 Robert P. Porter, *Life of William McKinley, Soldier, Lawyer, Statesman* (Cleveland: N. G. Hamilton Publishing Company, 1896), 48.

36 Bergeron, 66.

37 William Corby, *Memoirs of Chaplain Life: Three Years with the Irish Brigade in the Army of the Potomac* (Notre Dame, IN: Scholastic Press, 1894), 41.

37 Corby, 40–41.

37 Ibid., 41.

37 Albert T. Goodloe, "The Grayback Was an Undisputed Success," in Rod Gregg, *The Illustrated Confederate Reader* (New York: Gramercy Books, 1989), 32–33.

38–39 Gerrish, 49.

39 Austin Flint, ed., *Contributions Relating to the Causation and Prevention of Disease and to Camp Diseases* (New York: U.S. Sanitary Commission, 1867), 8.

40 Gerrish, 47.

41 James G. Hollandsworth Jr., *The Louisiana Native Guards: The Black Military Experience during the Civil War* (Baton Rouge: Louisiana State University Press, 1995), 98.

41 Corby, 41.

42 Gerrish, 20.

43 Ibid.

44 Jaqueline Beverly Stanard, letter to mother, May 12, 1864, Stanard Papers, Preston Library, Virginia Military Institute.

44 Ibid.

44 McCarthy, 45.

44 John H. Worsham, "Marching Along at a Brisk Rate," in Rod Gregg, *The Illustrated Confederate Reader* (New York: Gramercy Books, 1989), 28.

45 Gerrish, 25.

47 Corby, 34–35.

47 George F. Williams, *Bullet and Shell* (New York: Fords, Howard, & Hulbert, 1884), 199.

47 McCarthy, 55.

48 William C. Davis, *Battle at Bull Run* (New York: Doubleday & Company, 1977), 178.

48 Rhodes, 26.

48 Davis, 178.

49 Sam R. Watkins, *Co. Aytch: A Side Show of the Big Show* (New York: Collier, 1962), 42.

49–50 John T. Bell, *Tramps and Triumphs of the Second Iowa Infantry* (Omaha: Gibson, Miller & Richardson, 1886), 17.

50 Williams, 98.

51 Stephen W. Sears, *Landscape Turned Red* (New York: Warner Books, 1983), 233.

53 Corby, 132.

54 Beyer, W. F. and O. F. Keydel, eds., *Deeds of Valor: How America's*

Civil War Heroes Won the Medal of Honor (Detroit: Perrien-Keydel Co., 1903), 240.

54 Gerrish, 162.

55 Ibid.

55–56 Beyer, 334.

57 John S. Wise, *The End of an Era* (Boston: Houghton, Mifflin and Company, 1901), 346.

57 Ibid., 349.

57 Robert K. Beecham, *As If It Were Glory* (Madison, WI: Madison House, 1998), 183–84.

58 Floyd, 80.

59 Beyer, 115.

59 Ibid.

61 Ibid., 148.

61 Ibid., 214.

62 Ibid., 159.

62–63 Ibid., 258–259.

63 Ibid., 293.

64 Ibid., 32.

66 Gerrish, 166–167.

66 Ibid.

66–67 Ibid., 169.

67 William C. Oates, *The War Between the Union and the Confederacy* (New York: Neale Publishing Company, 1905), 226.

68 Ibid., 227.

69–70 William Howell Reed, *Hospital Life in the Army of the Potomac* (Boston: William V. Spencer, 1866), 57.

72 Bellard, 275.

73 William D. Wilkins, "Forgotten in the 'Black Hole': A Diary from Libby Prison," *Civil War Times Illustrated*, June 1976, 37.

73 Gerrish, 166–167.

73 Wilkins, 37.

74 Holland Thompson, ed., *The Photographic History of the Civil War*, (1911: repr., Edison, NJ: Blue and Grey Press, 1987) sec. 2, 4:14.

76 Ward, 338.

77 U.S. War Department, ser. 1, 27:92–93.

77 Ibid., ser. 2, 8:337.

77 Ibid., ser. 2, 5:216.

78 Berlin, 106–108.

80 Corby, 90.

80 Ibid., 90–91.

80 Ibid., 92.

81 Gerrish, 28.

82 Beyer, 343.

82–83 Rhodes, 164.

84 Wise, *The End of an Era*, 307.

84 John S. Wise, letter to Mrs. Ellen Bankhead Stanard, May 19, 1864, Stanard Papers, Preston Library, Virginia Military Institute.

85 McCarthy, 211–212.

86 Wise, *The End of an Era*, 427.

86 Mrs. Burton Harrison [Constance Cary], *Recollections, Grave and Gay* (New York: Charles Scribner's Sons, 1911), 207.

86–87 LaSalle Corbell Pickett, *Pickett and His Men* (Atlanta: Foote & Davies Company, 1899), 2.

88 Wise, *The End of an Era*, 427.

88 McCarthy, 128.

88 Richard Wheeler, *Witness to Appomattox* (New York: HarperCollins Publishers, 1989), 148.

89 McCarthy, 140.

89 U.S. War Department, ser. 1, 46:1267.

89 Ibid.

90 Ibid.

90–91 McCarthy, 153.

91 Gerrish, 266.

91 Ibid., 261.

92 Allen, 167.

93 Gerrish, 369.

93–94 McCarthy, 191.

94–95 Gerrish, 298–299.

96 Peggy Robbins, "The Glory Years," *Civil War Times Illustrated*, September/October 1994, 55.

96 McCarthy, 193.

96 Gerrish, 369.

97 James W. Wensyel, "Return to Gettysburg," *American History Illustrated*, July/August 1993, 50.

98 Brian Pohanka, letter to the author, March 3, 1999.

99 Gerrish, 371.

Selected Bibliography

Allen, Thomas B. *The Blue and the Gray.* Washington, DC: National Geographic Society, 1992.

Beecham, Robert K. *As If It Were Glory.* Madison, WI: Madison House, 1998.

Bell, John T. *Tramps and Triumphs of the Second Iowa Infantry.* Omaha: Gibson, Miller & Richardson, 1886.

Bellard, Alfred. *Gone for a Soldier.* Boston: Little, Brown and Company, 1975.

Bergeron, Arthur W., Jr. *The Civil War Reminiscences of Major Silas T. Grisamore, C.S.A.* Baton Rouge: Louisiana State University Press, 1993.

Berlin, Ira, ed. *Freedom's Soldiers: The Black Military Experience in the Civil War.* Cambridge: Cambridge University Press, 1998.

Beyer, Walter F., and O. F. Leydel, eds. *Deeds of Valor: How America's Civil War Heroes Won the Medal of Honor.* Detroit: Perrien-Keydel Co., 1903.

Bircher, William. *A Drummer-Boy's Diary: Comprising Four Years of Service with the Second Regiment Minnesota Veteran Volunteers, 1861–1865.* Saint Paul: St. Paul Book and Stationery Company, 1889.

Congdon, Don. *Combat: The Civil War.* New York: Mallard Press, 1967.

Corby, William. *Memoirs of Chaplain Life: Three Years with the Irish Brigade in the Army of the Potomac.* Notre Dame, IN: Scholastic Press, 1894.

Davis, William C. *Battle at Bull Run.* New York: Doubleday & Company, Inc., 1977.

Flint, Austin, ed. *Contributions Relating to the Causation and Prevention of Disease and to Camp Diseases.* New York: U.S. Sanitary Commission, 1867.

Floyd, Dale E. *The Letters and Diary of Thomas James Owen, Fiftieth New York Volunteer Engineer Regiment, during the Civil War.* Washington, DC: U.S. Government Printing Office, 1985.

Gerrish, Theodore. *Army Life: A Private's Reminiscences of the Civil War.* Portland, ME: Hoyt, Fogg & Donham, 1882.

Gregg, Rod. *The Illustrated Confederate Reader.* New York: Gramercy Books, 1989.

Haley, John W. *The Rebel Yell & the Yankee Hurrah.* Camden, ME: Down East Books, 1985.

Harrison, Mrs. Burton [Constance Cary]. *Recollections, Grave and Gay*. New York: Charles Scribner's Sons, 1911.

Hollandsworth, James G., Jr. *The Louisiana Native Guards: The Black Military Experience during the Civil War*. Baton Rouge: Louisiana State University Press, 1995.

Macdonald, John. *Great Battles of the Civil War*. New York: Collier Books, 1988.

McCarthy, Carlton. *Detailed Minutiae of Soldier Life in the Army of Northern Virginia, 1861–1865*. Richmond: Carlton McCarthy and Company, 1882.

Norton, Oliver W. *Army Letters 1861–1865*. Chicago: O. L. Deming, 1903.

Oates, Stephen B. *With Malice Toward None*. New York: New American Library, 1977.

Oates, William C. *The War Between the Union and the Confederacy*. New York: Neale Publishing Company, 1905.

Pickett, LaSalle Corbell. *Pickett and His Men*. Atlanta: Foote & Davies Company, 1899.

Reed, William Howell. *Hospital Life in the Army of the Potomac*. Boston: William V. Spencer, 1866.

Rhodes, Elisha Hunt. *All for the Union*. New York: Orion Books, 1985.

Sears, Stephen W. *Landscape Turned Red*. New York: Warner Books, 1983.

"Stanard Papers." Preston Library. Virginia Military Institute.

Thompson, Holland, ed. *The Photographic History of the Civil War*. 1911. Reprint, Edison, NJ: Blue and Grey Press, 1987.

U.S. Department of War. *War of the Rebellion: A Compilation of the Official Records of the Union and Confederate Armies*. Washington, DC: Government Printing Office, 1890–1901.

Wakeman, Sarah Rosetta. *An Uncommon Soldier*. New York: Oxford University Press, 1994.

Ward, Geoffrey C. *The Civil War*. New York: Alfred A. Knopf, 1990.

Watkins, Sam R. *Co. Aytch: A Side Show of the Big Show*. New York: Collier, 1962.

Welsh, Peter. *Irish Green and Union Blue*. New York: Fordham University Press, 1986.

Wheeler, Richard. *Witness to Appomattox*. New York: HarperCollins Publishers, 1989.

Wiley, Bell Irvin. *The Life of Billy Yank*. New York: Doubleday & Company, 1952.

Wilkinson, Warren. *Mother, May You Never See the Sights I Have Seen*. New York: William Morrow, 1990.

Williams, George F. *Bullet and Shell*. New York: Fords, Howard, & Hulbert, 1884.

Wise, John S. *The End of an Era*. Boston: Houghton, Mifflin and Company, 1901.

FURTHER INFORMATION AND WEBSITES

BOOKS

Arnold, James R. *The Civil War*. Minneapolis: Twenty-First Century Books, 2005.

Arnold, James R., and Roberta Wiener. The Civil War (six-book series). Minneapolis: Lerner Publications Company, 2002.

Beller, Susan Provost. *Medical Practices in the Civil War*. Charlotte, VT: OurStory, 1992.

Brill, Marlene Targ. *Diary of a Drummer Boy*. Minneapolis: First Avenue Editions, 1998.

Damon, Duane. *Growing Up in the Civil War: 1860 to 1864*. Minneapolis: Lerner Publications Company, 2003.

Day, Nancy. *Your Travel Guide to Civil War America*. Minneapolis: First Avenue Editions, 2001.

Egger-Bovet, Howard. *Book of the American Civil War*. Boston: Little, Brown & Co., 1998.

Paulsen, Gary. *Soldier's Heart: Being the Story of the Enlistment and Due Service of the Boy Charley Goddard in the First Minnesota Volunteers*. New York: Delacorte, 1998.

Roberts, Jeremy. *Abraham Lincoln*. Minneapolis: Twenty-First Century Books, 2004.

Silverman, Jerry. *Songs and Stories of the Civil War*. Minneapolis: Twenty-First Century Books, 2002.

Steenwyk, Elizabeth van. *Seneca Chief, Army General: A Story about Ely Parker*. Minneapolis: Millbrook Press, 2001.

Sullivan, George. *The Civil War at Sea*. Minneapolis: Twenty-First Century Books, 2001.

Walker, Sally M. *Secrets of a Civil War Submarine: Solving the Mystery of the H. L. Hunley*. Minneapolis: Carolrhoda Books, Inc., 2005.

Zeinert, Karen. *Those Courageous Women of the Civil War*. Minneapolis: Twenty-First Century Books, 1998.

CD-ROMS AND DVDS

American Heritage. *The Civil War: The Complete Multimedia Experience*. New York: Simon & Schuster Interactive, 1995.

Glory, DVD, directed by Edward Zwick (Culver City: Sony Pictures, 1998).

WEBSITES

CivilWar@Smithsonian
http://www.civilwar.si.edu/home.html
This website associated with the Smithsonian, a museum in Washington, D.C., has a timeline, a discussion of the issues that divided the nation, as

well as a collection of photographs and interpretations of Civil War items from the Smithsonian collections.

The Civil War Home Page
http://www.civil-war.net/
Visitors to the Civil War Home Page can browse in one of the largest and most comprehensive collections of Civil War related material available on the Internet. This is a clearinghouse site that attempts to link to all Civil War material anywhere on the web.

The Civil War Preservation Trust
http://www.civilwar.org/
The website of the Civil War Preservation Trust offers visitors many ways to learn about and enjoy the nation's Civil War history, from games and books to location of battlefields and reenactments. The organization leads the effort to purchase and preserve Civil War sites before they are lost forever to development.

The Library of Congress Selected Civil War Photographs
http://memory.loc.gov/ammem/cwphtml/cwphome.html
The Library of Congress in Washington, D.C., holds a wonderful collection of more than 1,100 original photographs from the time of the Civil War and other memorabilia. Through this website, visitors can see a selection of portraits, browse a timeline, and learn how photographers worked in the field.

The National Archives
http://www.nara.gov
The National Archives is a vast collection of information about the people involved in the Civil War. Visitors to the website can search service and pension records, look at photos, and conduct all kinds of research

The National Civil War Museum
http://www.nationalcivilwarmuseum.org/
The National Civil War Museum is located in Harrisburg, Pennsylvania. Its website gives information about this comprehensive museum, which opened in 2001.

National Park Service, The American Civil War Homepage
http://cwar.nps.gov/civilwar/
Operated by the National Park Service, this website helps people interested in visiting Civil War battlefields plan their trip. It also has a timeline and links to other Civil War sites. It also hosts the Soldiers and Sailors System, a database of men and women who actually fought in the Civil War

PBS: The Civil War
http://www.pbs.org/civilwar/
This comprehensive website is tied to the landmark Ken Burns television series about the Civil War that aired in 1990. The site features maps and photographs, timelines, biographies, and more.

INDEX

About the Author

Susan Provost Beller is the author of twenty history books for young readers. She writes from her home in Charlotte, Vermont, when she is not either traveling to see historic sites or visiting with her three children and five grandchildren. Her one wish is that someone would invent a time machine so she could go back and really see the past!

Photo Acknowledgments

The images in this book are used with the permission of: Library of Congress, pp. 2 (LC-DIG-cwpb-01730), 10 (LC-DIG-cwpb-02020), 12 (LC-DIG-cwpb-04292), 27 (LC-DIG-cwpb-01311), 29 (LC-B8184-10548), 33 (LC-DIG-cwpb-01730), 34 (LC-B8184-4350), 38 (LC-DIG-cwpb-00280), 46 (LC-DIG-cwpb-03748), 49 (LC-USZC4-1910), 51 (LC-DIG-cwpb-00240), 53 (LC-B4821-6704), 55 (LC-DIG-cwpbh-03386), 63 (LC-USZ61-7824), 68 (LC-B8184-B-605), 69 (LC-DIG-cwpb-03950), 82 (LC-B8184-40497), 87 (LC-B811-3242), 90 (LC-DIG-cwpb-03908); The Library of Virginia, p. 8; Wisconsin Historical Society, WHi-1909, p. 13; Research Division of the Oklahoma Historical Society, p. 14; © Robert Burke, p. 16; National Archives, pp. 19, 26, 43, 50, 56, 60, 67, 76, 78, 81, 94; Minnesota Historical Society, pp. 20, 42; Collection of the Dyer Library/Saco Museum, Saco, Maine, p. 23; Vermont Historical Society, pp. 30, 40, 45; Used by permission from The Wm McKinley Presidential Library and Museum, Canton, Ohio, p. 36; © CORBIS, pp. 52, 97; © Richard A. Dorbin, www.paragonlight.com, p. 61; © Sam Abell/National Geographic Society Image Collection, p. 65; © Bettmann/CORBIS, p. 70; The Western Reserve Historical Society, Cleveland, Ohio, p. 72; Mathew B. Brady, Minnesota Historical Society, p. 74; Courtesy of the Georgia Department of Archives and History, p. 84; © North Wind Picture Archives, p. 92; © Getty Images, p. 98. Map by © Laura Westlund/Independent Picture Service, backgrounds, p. 100.

Cover: © Connie Toops (statue), © Laura Westlund/Independent Picture Service (map).